# CHRISTMAS IN THE SUN

Sapphire Cay, book 4

RJ SCOTT

MEREDITH RUSSELL

Love Lane Books

# Copyright

Christmas in the Sun (Sapphire Cay 4)

## All Rights Reserved

## Dedication

*For our family and friends*

SAPPHIRE CAY 4

# CHRISTMAS IN THE *Sun*

## RJ SCOTT & MEREDITH RUSSELL

# Chapter One

*KILL ME NOW.* LUCAS CLOSED HIS EYES, COUNTED TO three, and hoped the chaos of the morning would have vanished when he opened them. The Lambert wedding had been their largest to date. Dylan and Scott had already headed out with the first boatload of guests and were due to return within the hour. Not soon enough as far as Lucas was concerned. He hit three in his count but couldn't bring himself to open his eyes as he heard a squeal accompanied by something smashing.

*Not the vase. Please not the vase.* The jade-colored ornamental pot thing had belonged to his grandmother, and though he thought it was pretty damn ugly, it still held a place in his heart.

He opened his eyes to find his grandma's vase still sitting on the table in the entrance. He looked beyond it at the last of the Lamberts' party. There were eight guests left in the hotel, four of whom were...*kids*. He wasn't sure he'd say he hated them, just that he wasn't predisposed with the nurturing instinct to deal with energetic youngsters. When their parents had died, Tasha had been seventeen. She had been well on the way to having her own life, and his input had mostly become about his career and money as a means of supporting her.

The parent of the child closest to the terracotta pot that had been knocked over and now lay in several pieces on the floor reprimanded her son and looked apologetically toward Lucas. Before Lucas could muster the energy to deal with the broken pottery, Agnes, their housekeeper, appeared from out of nowhere, shooing the children away as she picked up the pieces of the pot and put them into a black bag. Lucas mouthed her a *thank you*.

"Everything okay?" Jamie said from behind him.

Lucas glanced over his shoulder and nodded. Everybody was checked out. It was just a case of waiting for Dylan to return with the *Liberty*. "Give it twenty and then we'll usher them down to the pier."

"Cool," Jamie said. He rested his elbows on the front desk. "Edward's waiting it out in his room." He smirked as he gazed across the foyer. "Kids are apparently sticky."

Laughing, Lucas rubbed at his shoulder. "Some are." Tasha had had a friend back in college who'd had a little boy. Lucas came home one evening to find the pair visiting Tasha. The first thing the three-year-old boy had done was run up to Lucas and hug his leg, leaving a greasy handprint on his pants.

"I'm tempted to tell him I want to adopt just to see the look on his face."

Lucas could only imagine how Edward would cope with fitting something as unpredictable as a child into his routines. A full-on meltdown was likely. "Start easy. Maybe fish."

Jamie laughed and checked the time. "They should be on their way back by now. Did you discuss plans for a second boat yet?"

"New boat," Lucas pointed out. A new, bigger boat was what Lucas had in mind, but Dylan was being incredibly stubborn over the *Lady Liberty*. It had gotten to the stage that not even a fresh coat of paint could disguise just how tired the *Liberty* was. Scott had worked on the old engine more and more in recent months, and Lucas waited for the day where sticking the proverbial Band-Aid on would no longer be good enough.

"You'll never get him to part with *Liberty*," Jamie stated. "I know it. You know it. Dominiq knows it."

Lucas pressed his lips in a line and distracted himself from the sudden rise in noise with trying to figure out who was older, Dominiq or the *Liberty*. Fondness for the chef warmed his chest. He'd be sad to see him go at the end of the season. But it seemed Dominiq would be leaving the kitchen in equally capable hands. Adam had proved to be a breath of fresh air. The man was just as passionate about his food and organic produce, but he brought with him youth and his own ideas. It was interesting to watch the two men work together. Like a well-oiled machine, they knew exactly how to work as a team, each doing what they needed to produce exquisite meals for their guests. Everyone would miss Dominiq in the kitchen and the man himself was irreplaceable. He was like this huge teddy bear, good for a hug, but also wise and fatherly.

"Mommy, potty." The youngest of the four children who had been running in crazy airplane circles stopped and did a strange dance.

"I need to get some air," Lucas said. He patted Jamie on the back. "Hold the fort." He didn't give Jamie a chance to object before he moved from behind the front desk and headed outside.

Taking a deep breath, Lucas looked out across the beach and to the sea. He squinted, looking for *Lady Liberty* on the horizon. He couldn't wait for the wedding party to leave so they could start on their own plans for the holidays. He took the few steps to the path and then started a slow walk around the hotel. He couldn't believe it was already the twenty-third of December. It seemed like just yesterday they were making plans to spend Christmas with friends and family. The Lamberts had opted for a white Christmas and had planned the second part of their honeymoon back in Vermont, which had given him and Dylan the opportunity to have a wedding-free Christmas for the first time in three years, with the next wedding not booked in until the thirtieth for the New Year.

Lucas took a right and detoured into what was now commonly known as Scott's Garden. Scott had worked incredibly hard the last two seasons in order to get the overgrown garden back under control. He had cleared the paths from weeds, thinned out the borders, and trimmed back the trees. Flowers bloomed in a rainbow's worth of colors, interspersed with the simple beauty of white blossoms. Lucas knew very little about plants and soil and shade, but he could appreciate the effort Scott had put in to make the garden as beautiful as it was.

Checking the time, he made his way through the garden and around the back of the hotel. Tasha and Liam's flight would get in soon. They had caught up in August as they always did when he and Dylan returned to the mainland for a short while during the stormy season in the Bahamas. She had looked good, and there was no doubt she and Liam were as much in love as the day they married. Lucas was glad to be able to spend Christmas Day with her this year.

Lucas stopped on the patio and glanced at the hotel. He couldn't see much through the sliding doors because of the reflection of the sun, but he could make out the low din of what he guessed was the sound of the children still playing.

Should he feel bad he had left Jamie in there alone? Yes. Did he? Hell, no. Lucas was sure he'd earned ten minutes of peace after the morning from hell. If it wasn't children running circles round him, it was the adults in the party—a lost wedding band in twelve, guests expecting breakfast despite being almost an hour late, and the kleptomaniac in nine. Who would want to try and steal a kettle? He closed his eyes and rubbed the back of his neck. He smiled as he fingered the hair at his collar.

He wore his hair longer these days. For him it was a way to embrace his new life. He may be the levelheaded, often seen as the more boring of the pair of him and Dylan, but he was enjoying the freedom Sapphire Cay offered. No set hours, no ulcers, no stress. He sighed inwardly as he corrected himself. Some stress. It just wasn't the same day-after-day pressure he'd experienced in his former life in contracts management. Here he had a life that wasn't work, work, work twenty-four seven. He was tanned and healthy and slept peacefully each night beside the man he loved. The man he'd one day call husband.

Sunlight caught the silver band on his right hand. They hadn't set a date yet, always too busy making other people's dreams come true. Besides, there was no rush. He was happy as he was. They both were. They had committed to each other, had everything they needed. Their lives were perfect and switching a ring from his right hand to his left wasn't going to change how much they loved each other.

Lucas jumped as there was a bang on the patio door. Oh dear. Jamie was pressed up against the window, his face squashed and his hands flat on the glass. Lucas quirked an eyebrow and watched as Jamie slid downward, a child at each leg squealing with delight. Lucas smirked. At least someone was enjoying themselves.

"You'll be cleaning that," he said and pointed at the smudged window.

Jamie leaned back and cupped his ears.

"The window," Lucas said slowly and loudly. He pointed again and this time Jamie shrugged and grinned before being dragged away by the playing children. Lucas sighed. His gaze drifted to the gazebo standing a little way down from the patio and pool. Had they really trusted Jamie with rebuilding that? He laughed to himself and then headed toward the kitchen.

"Good morning," Dominiq said cheerfully as Lucas stepped through the door into the back of the kitchen. "How are we this fine day?" If Lucas didn't know better, he'd think Dominiq had been at the rum.

Lucas leaned back against the edge of the kitchen counter. "I'm great."

"How are our guests?"

"Still here."

Dominiq laughed. "I look forward to sharing a boat ride with them." He wiped his hands on his apron and then untied it. "So, we've prepped what we can for your dinner. Should help Adam out a little. He'll make everything else fresh on the day."

"Thanks," Lucas said. "You are still welcome to join us if you want to. Your family, too."

Shaking his head, Dominiq folded his apron and placed it on one of the breakfast bar stools. "I need to start to pull away. Break the ties." He flashed a smile. "Hard enough thinking of leaving this place without settling in for a cozy Christmas."

"There's an easy solution to that," Lucas said.

"And what's that?" Dominiq asked.

"Don't leave." Since coming to the island, Dominiq had made it so easy and comfortable. As far as Lucas was concerned, Dominiq *was* Sapphire Cay and everything it stood for.

Dominiq chuckled. "Not sure young Adam would agree." At that moment the door swung open and Adam walked in. He stopped as Lucas and Dominiq both looked at him.

"What?" Adam said and glanced over his shoulder as the door shut behind him.

"Talking about you, not to you," Dominiq chimed. He gave Adam a big grin.

Adam seemed confused but shook it off and carried

on. "I've got the list you wanted. Claude should have it all boxed up and ready for you, but if you can just check everything off for me that would great."

"You ever cooked a turkey?" Lucas asked, taking the list and reading over the first few items. The ink smelled fresh and the paper was still warm from the printer.

"Not one to feed eight. Have you?" Adam asked. His eyes held a playful sparkle.

Lucas looked at Adam and color heated Adam's cheeks. Lucas couldn't help but grin. The man had grown in confidence since joining them at the hotel fulltime. He'd even taken the brave step of questioning one of Edward's table arrangements last month. Lucas doubted he would again. Adam had learned his lesson with that one.

"Adam will do just fine," Dominiq said proudly.

"I know he will," Lucas said. He'd seen the dishes Adam had produced alongside Dominiq and also alone. He was sure Adam would do a great job. Lucas just wanted everything to be perfect. He hadn't spent Christmas Day with Tasha in a long time. Even when he was back in his former life he always seemed to be distracted with work. "Just came over a little *Edwardy* there for a minute." He glanced at his watch. "You about ready, Dom?"

"Sure. Just need to get my bags."

"Okay. See you on the pier in twenty." Lucas left Adam and Dominiq to finish up and headed back to the foyer. Stepping out of the kitchen, he stopped, closed his eyes, and shook his head. Lucas opened his eyes and stared at the scene. Jamie was lying on the floor bench-pressing one of the boys. Muscles rippled in Jamie's strong arms as he lifted the boy up in the air, and the boy squirmed and kicked his legs as if he were swimming in some invisible sea. Lucas sighed and made his way to the front desk. Would this morning never end?

## Chapter Two

DYLAN WATCHED LUCAS WAVE THE LAST OF THE Lamberts to their limo and grinned in support when Lucas turned and faced him and let his game face drop in exhaustion. For very understandable reasons, this last wedding had been hard on Lucas. Dylan expected it was a combination of kids and that whole end-of-the-year feeling, and he'd said so to Lucas this morning. Both agreed they were lucky that they had no wedding over Christmas and now had days in front of them to chill with family and friends.

Lucas walked over, and as he walked he became more relaxed. It was intriguing to watch. What wasn't so cool was that Lucas was rubbing his stomach, and not for the first time, Dylan was concerned about the whole ulcer thing. Too many weddings in succession. They didn't need to do as many, and he resolved to talk about it to his fiancé when they got back to Sapphire Cay and had some quiet time. They needed to pick up Adam's order from Claude but then had time to kill before Tasha and Liam arrived in Marsh Harbor. After that, it was back to the island to relax.

"You ready to go find Claude and the order?" Lucas asked. Dylan immediately stood and pulled his lover in close.

"You okay?" he asked quickly.

Lucas huffed a breath and buried his face in Dylan's hair. "Tired," he said. "I think we should make the island for adults only," he added. Then he yawned widely. Dylan chuckled.

"Nah," he began. "You'd miss all those sticky chocolate fingers and all that running around like mad from the little people."

"I promise you I wouldn't."

Hand in hand, they strolled from the harbor and into the small town. Their order was ready in boxes, and due to the fact Adam appeared to have ordered enough food for an army, they borrowed a wheelbarrow and transported it down to the *Liberty*. Dylan jumped down into the boat, and one by one Lucas passed down the boxes. Dylan tied them in a balanced pattern around the boat, leaving room for his passengers to sit with their luggage, even though Lucas had told him Tasha said she was just bringing a bikini.

"I'll go get a table," Lucas called down. He didn't

really need to get a table; the café was small but there was always space. This side of the harbor was quiet and mostly for locals.

"Ice cream," Dylan shouted back. "Give me five."

He fiddled with straps, then stood back to look at the balance of the *Liberty*. He was experienced at fitting everything in after years of doing this job. Proud of his boat, he checked out *Liberty* and ignored the peeling paint on the stern and the worn wood of the pilot station. She'd weathered storms and heat, and she'd done well. Lucas had valid points as to why they should replace her, but Dylan couldn't get his head around them. Well, apart from the luxury aspect. Lucas's argument that people paid a lot of money for Sapphire Cay was easily countered by Dylan's assertion that they would expect Caribbean rustic.

"He'll make me replace you, girl," Dylan muttered. "One day, you know, but we'll fight it." It didn't strike him as odd that he was talking to a boat, but equally he hoped no one spotted him. With a sigh of resignation that this was probably *Liberty*'s last season, he climbed the ladder and up onto the harbor wall. The café was a few feet away, and from here they could watch the boats and kill time waiting for Tasha and Liam. And to top it off he would finally get to try Scott's recommended chocolate ice cream sundae.

Lucas was already at a rickety table and slumped back in the chair with his eyes closed, and Dylan bypassed him to order the ice cream concoction and a cold drink of lemonade for his fiancé. Lucas needed something to cool him down and at the same time refresh him.

"With ya in a few," the assistant said in a sing-song voice. "Take ya table," he added with a wide grin.

Dylan crossed to Lucas and peered over the edge to check on *Liberty*. She sat, slowly moving in the gentle motion of the sea.

"Okay?" Lucas asked on another yawn.

"She's fine," Dylan said. He regretted saying it this way as soon as Lucas raised a single eyebrow in question. Instead of the usual teasing, Dylan decided to head it off at the pass. "When're Tasha and Liam in?"

Lucas moved his head back to peer up at the sky. He'd not worn a watch since he'd decided to stay with Dylan. Even now Dylan was pleased to see Lucas was getting good at judging the time by how he felt— hungry, tired, or by the position of the sun in the sky or even the scents of the day in the air. Dylan loved that a small part of Lucas was relaxing, and he just wished Lucas would let that final knot of constant concern unravel in his chest.

Lucas frowned. "An hour." He was clearly guessing. "Told them to meet us here."

"I ordered you lemonade," Dylan said.

"I wanted coffee," Lucas protested.

Dylan wasn't going to argue. Lucas hadn't entirely

cut down his coffee use, but he needed to be careful.

"Saw you rubbing your stomach," Dylan said.

Lucas looked down at himself, and his eyes widened when he realized he was still doing it. Quickly, he moved his hand, but not before the damage had been done.

"I don't know why..." he began. "I'm just tired. I got the all clear. I'm relaxing, I feel good."

Dylan reached over and grasped Lucas's other hand. "Let's keep it that way, then." He shuffled his chair closer and kissed Lucas firmly. He could sit here all day kissing Lucas. All day. A noise, shouting, barking, separated them, and Dylan glanced over at the intrusion into what had been a very nice kiss. He couldn't see anything, but the barking had turned to whining and the shouts to laughter.

"Keep an eye on *Liberty*," he said, and then before Lucas could say a word, Dylan was out of his seat and heading behind the café where the alleys converged to one single point with bins and recycling. At first he couldn't see what was happening because a group of young kids were like a wall surrounding whatever was going on.

Then his height gave him the advantage, and he could see a dog cowering in the space between crates. One of the boys was poking it with a stick. He didn't actually poke the dog each time, but clearly this had gone on for some time.

"Told ya he'd stop barking if we scared 'im," the young boy said with a laugh. The rest of the group joined in with *yays*, although Dylan noticed a few were looking around fearfully and not really joining in.

"We should leave 'im," one of those who wasn't grinning like an idiot said.

Dylan waded in. "I think that's a good idea," he said firmly. He pushed himself between the kids and the dog. For a second Dylan thought he saw defiance in the kid with the stick—the thought process telegraphed on his face about whether he should poke Dylan. A simple move and the stick was in Dylan's hand.

"What's your name?" he asked. He wasn't really expecting a reply. True to what he thought would happen, the kid sneered and scarpered along with his little friends. A few of the kids, the ones who hadn't joined in, hovered uncertainly.

"Whose dog is this?" he asked them. They looked at each other as if they were weighing up what to say. "Whose dog?" he said again.

"No one's," one of the smallest kids said. "He's on his own."

"A stray?" Dylan summarized.

"Yes."

The kids dispersed without a backward glance. Seemed like now that an adult was here, they could leave the dog alone. Dylan spun on his foot and faced the dog. It appeared to be a mix, something between a terrier and an English bulldog. He couldn't see any injuries, but the poor thing was painfully thin and his eyes downcast. Dylan moved and then cursed when the dog cowered and he realized he still had the damn stick in his hands. He carefully placed it where the dog could see what he had done, then gently went to his knees. The dog didn't look rabid, and there was no sign of blood anywhere. He held out a hand but the dog shrank back instead of sniffing him.

"Damn stray," the owner of the café snapped. He stood at the rear exit of the café with a basket of scraps and rubbish. He tipped the whole lot in a bin and cursed again. "Nothing but trouble, in my trash."

"He's probably hungry," Dylan suggested reasonably.

"That's maybe right, but I ain't gonna feed him," he said. "I got kids to feed first."

Dylan didn't want to ask if it was his kids that were poking at the dog. "Pass me some of the scraps," he ordered. Reaching into his pocket, he pulled out a twenty and handed it up to the café owner. "I'll pay for some meat and bread. Nothing too fatty or heavy. And a bowl of water."

The café owner cursed and blustered, but he did as he was asked. Seemed money spoke here. Dylan watched the dog until he was sure the poor thing had eaten something and drunk some water. Then he patted it on the head and smiled when it pushed up into his hand. It didn't wag its tail, but the butting of his head into Dylan's hand was a sure sign that Dylan had done something right.

Torn, he knew he had to go back to Lucas, but at the corner he turned back to see the dog. It had gone. Disappeared. He should be pleased it wasn't hanging about waiting for the kids to come back, but a part of him was sad that it had just gone.

When he got back, Lucas looked up from his lemonade. "Where'd you go?"

"Some kids were beating up on a dog. Poor thing."

"Is it okay?" Lucas asked, concerned.

"Yeah, he's gone now."

Lucas tilted his head. "Did he have a white nose, with dark ears, pathetic eyes, and was kind of on the skinny side?"

"Yeah," Dylan replied. "How did you…?" Catching on, he realized the dog was sitting next to him leaning against his chair, and hell, was that a wag in his tail?

"Seems like you've got a friend."

"He's a stray," Dylan explained. He patted the dog's head again, and this time he was rewarded by two wags of the little tail.

"What kind of dog is it?" Lucas asked with a frown. "Some kind of cross?"

"Maybe a mix way back. It's a boy." He scratched between the dog's ears and smiled down at it.

"Probably got fleas and all sorts."

"Seems pretty clean," Dylan said. "Just really thin and a little undomesticated."

Lucas shook his head. "No," he said firmly.

"No, what?"

"No, we don't need a dog on the island."

Dylan immediately felt defensive. "I didn't say anything."

Lucas smiled. "Not in words."

"I know we don't need a dog," Dylan said carefully. "Hell, imagine if it was all up in the guests' faces? Edward would have a cow if it caused chaos at a wedding. It would undoubtedly jump in the pool as well." Dylan said all this, but all he could see was dark brown eyes looking up at him with adoration. He had to be sensible. "Shoo," he finally said. "Off you go."

At first the dog stared and didn't move, but then with what looked like a huff of disappointment, it strolled away without a backward glance.

"We could get a cat maybe," Lucas consoled him.

"I don't like cats much," Dylan said. "I always wanted a dog. Not that one though," he hastened to add.

"You're right," Lucas agreed, although he had the same expression on his face that he often got when Dylan talked about his childhood—or lack of it. Kind of a combination of sadness and understanding.

"Lucas!" The name being called from across the way had Lucas standing and crossing to his sister in an instant. Dylan stayed where he was so he could watch over *Liberty* but was soon part of hugs and kisses when Tasha and Liam joined them at the table. With hellos and laughter, they all made it onto the boat, and soon they had pulled away from the harbor and were on their way to Sapphire Cay. A bark caught Dylan's attention, and he looked back. The dog was standing on the wall looking down at them. The drop was maybe six feet and the dog appeared to be contemplating jumping. Dylan cut the engine in indecision as to what to do.

"You have got to be joking," Lucas said in disbelief at the dog and what it was possibly planning to do. Dylan couldn't agree with the sentiment more when, with a yip, the dog jumped in the water and disappeared below the surface.

"Jeez," Liam said instantly. "Is it okay?"

"Oh god, that poor dog," Tasha added.

It seemed like everyone was holding their collective breaths until abruptly the dog surfaced. As if it jumped six-foot walls into water every day, it began to paddle over to them. Dylan moved to the back of the boat between the luggage.

"What are you doing?" Lucas asked.

"It's swimming over."

Lucas looked at him with confusion in his eyes. Then realization flooded his expression followed quickly by acceptance and love.

"Best help him on board, then. Looks like we've got a dog."

## Chapter Three

THE BOAT RIDE BACK TO THE ISLAND HAD SEEMED longer than usual to Lucas. Along with guests and boxes, they had managed to pick up a dog, and Lucas wasn't entirely sure what they were going to do with the animal once they made it home to Sapphire Cay. The dog was friendly enough and had certainly been a source of amusement as it had chased itself in circles attempting to catch its tail. From the look in Tasha's eyes, his sister appeared to be as equally smitten with the dog as Dylan and had happily sat stroking it when it had finally settled down in the boat.

Tying off the boat, Dylan jumped back onto *Liberty* and picked up the first of the boxes. He smiled at Lucas before patting his leg and encouraging the dog to follow him.

"I am shattered," Tasha announced. She took her husband's hand as he helped her to her feet. "Is it okay if I'm antisocial for an hour or so?" She looked at Lucas. "I promise to be super fun after a nap."

Lucas laughed but his humor quickly turned to concern. "You do look a little pale. Are you okay?" Lucas asked.

Tasha nodded. "Just tired and I forgot how bumpy the ride over can be." She shrugged and Liam helped her onto the pier. She smiled at her husband, letting him go ahead with their things as she turned to wait for Lucas.

Grabbing the last of his sister's things, Lucas joined her on the pier. Lucas carried Tasha's bag as they headed toward the beach. He finally felt like he could just stop with all the work and the stress and start enjoying the holidays.

"He looks happy," Tasha said of the dog. The dog bounded across the sand, running in circles in front of Dylan.

The dog seemed to be enjoying itself. It wagged its tail and held its ears high as it stuck out its tongue, panting in the heat. The dog had the most beautiful brown eyes, all warm and soulful. Just what he needed, another set of big beautiful eyes giving him puppy looks day and night.

"Think we should call someone?" he asked.

"Like who?" Tasha asked. She slipped her hand in his as they walked.

Good question. The dog seemed to be a stray. No collar, hungry looking, and desperate for human love. By the looks of the animal, nobody had shown the dog care or extended their home to him in a long time. Lucas could see that. And if the dog did belong to somebody, Lucas figured he or she didn't deserve such a happy, devoted creature. The dog was incredibly affectionate, and he was surprised at how something so simple had made Dylan's eyes shine so brightly. It was quite possible his lover's heart had been stolen by the newest guest on the island.

"Maybe the cops?" she said. "Just to check no one's reported the poor thing missing or stolen."

"I guess," Lucas agreed. He smiled, noting how Dylan gently nudged the dog with his foot. With his hands full, Dylan was at risk of being tripped by the excitable animal. Lucas would call the police station in the morning, though he doubted anyone would look into it properly until after Christmas.

"Cheer up," Tasha said. She squeezed his hand. "I'm here for a few days of sun, sea, and Christmas fun with my big brother." She tugged on his arm until he stopped. "I've missed him."

Lucas smiled. "I missed you, too."

Her eyes held a smile. "You look good," she said.

"And I mean *really* good." She looked up at the hotel. "Every time I see you it amazes me how different things are, how much better."

Shyly, Lucas ducked his head. He smiled. "Let's get you and Liam settled," he said.

Tasha looked along the pier to where Liam was standing with the rest of their things. She smiled and then gazed back to the hotel. "I can't believe how long it's been since we got married here. It's still just as beautiful."

Lucas joined her in admiring the hotel and island. It *was* beautiful. He was so lucky to be able to call the place home.

"What the hell?" Jamie said with a laugh. He quirked an eyebrow, joining Lucas on the pier. "Where'd the dog come from?" He pointed his thumb to where Dylan had apparently given in, placing the boxes on the beach and crouching to pet the dog.

"Don't ask," Lucas said. "Long story."

"Oh, okay." Jamie smiled and turned to Tasha. "Jamie," he said. "We haven't met, right?"

"No, we haven't." Tasha held out her hand and smiled sweetly as Jamie took it. "But Lucas has talked about you. You're the previous owners' son and you're dating the wedding planner."

Jamie nodded. "That I am." He glanced over his shoulder. "You know Ed's gonna freak when he sees the mutt, right?"

Nodding, Lucas chewed on his lip. Despite the dog having the adorability factor, he wasn't sure the animal would suit life on the island and could only imagine what mischief and mayhem might follow. "Dylan will keep an eye on it."

"Uh-huh. Well, when my man has a meltdown, know I'm bringing him straight to you."

The image of Edward in the midst of a full freak-out was both amusing and unsettling. He considered how much trouble one animal could realistically cause. Poop, shedding hair, chewing and clawing, burying things, and unearthing plants in Scott's garden—Lucas really needed to discuss setting some rules for the animal with Dylan.

Jamie carried on past Lucas and jumped onto the *Liberty* to help with the unloading. "Oh," he called. Lucas looked back at him. Jamie was crouching beside an open box. "What are you planning on feeding him?"

"What?"

"The dog?" Jamie held up a fresh mango. "I don't suppose you bought any dog food while you were over there?"

Lucas opened his mouth and just as quickly shut it. He looked at Tasha, who simply smirked. "Just great," he said. He felt a headache coming on. He didn't need the added stress of suddenly being responsible for the dog and its welfare.

"I'm sure there'll be something we can feed it," Tasha insisted.

They had plenty of food on the island, but Lucas wasn't sure how Adam would feel about dishing the animal up some of the prime cuts of meat they'd collected from Claude, let alone carving the dog a slice off the Christmas turkey. "I'll talk to Adam and see what we can do," he decided. He knew there were things dogs shouldn't eat. Chocolate he remembered and was it dairy?

"I think Scott had a dog as a kid," Jamie said. He folded down the flaps of the box and got to his feet. Picking up the box, he found his footing before jumping back onto the pier. "You should get your lovely sister settled in, and I'll have Scott go talk to Adam. We can have a look on the internet, too. I think we should be safe with meat and veg though."

Tasha squeezed Lucas's hand and leaned in close, hugging him as she planted a kiss on his cheek. "See, problem solved." Had she sensed how tense he was feeling about being unprepared for the addition of a dog over Christmas? "It's Christmas. Relax. Have fun. Don't stress."

Lucas smiled. He could do that. He could be that guy and have fun, not worry. He looked across the beach in search of his lover. With a feeling of contentment, he met Dylan's eyes, but how Dylan seemed to shy away left Lucas just as suddenly cold.

Was Lucas's mind playing tricks on him? Had Dylan really turned away from him? Maybe the guilt of having his family near for the holidays had finally gotten to Lucas. Though he figured it was ridiculous, Lucas couldn't help but feel bad about shows of affection toward his sister and her husband. It wasn't a new feeling. Dylan had accompanied Lucas when he'd last visited Tasha. Even though Tasha smothered Dylan in an equal share of hugs and kisses, whenever she'd hugged Lucas or the siblings had shared some personal joke or moment, Lucas had felt awkward. He knew Dylan hadn't had the best time growing up, but hell, who of them had had the perfect childhood?

Tasha released Lucas from her hug as Dylan disappeared ahead of them. Lucas realized just how much he missed the comforting warmth of her hold. With a smile, he pressed a firm kiss to her cheek and headed toward the hotel.

It didn't take long to show Tasha and Liam to their room in the hotel and get them settled.

"If you need anything just holler," he said. Pulling the door closed behind him, he left the couple to themselves, giving them time to relax. They'd agreed to meet up later that afternoon on the patio.

On a mission, Lucas headed out to *Liberty*, collected the last of the boxes, and made his way to the kitchen. As he walked, Lucas could think of nothing and no one other than Dylan. Guilt weighed on Lucas's mind, and he came to the conclusion it was time to talk to his lover. He didn't want to say he had gone behind Dylan's back, but he'd made a choice about something and hadn't exactly told Dylan about it. In his experience, keeping secrets rarely ended in anything but tears. He needed to talk to Dylan, and he needed to do it today to stand any chance of enjoying the holidays or being able to dismiss the low ache of stress in his gut. Could guilt actually be eating away at his insides?

Taking a right, Lucas pushed against the kitchen door with his back. Reversing in, the door swung closed and he turned around. "What's the dog doing in here?" he asked, placing the box he had been carrying on the unit.

Dylan lowered his hand, allowing the dog to lick his fingers. "Don't worry. I'm keeping an eye on him," he said and patted the dog on the head.

"It's not him I'm worried about." He joined Dylan, Scott, Jamie, and Adam around the breakfast bar. Adam had already begun his inspection of the produce they'd collected from Claude.

"There's no one here who'd go telling tales," Adam said. "Besides, before Dominiq gets back, this kitchen will be as spotless as the big man left it."

Lucas looked at the dog. The last thing he needed was someone finding a dog hair in their wedding breakfast. "Okay. But someone needs to give him a bath."

"Don't worry. Scott will fix him a bath later," Dylan said.

"Huh," Scott said. He wore a clueless expression on his face and already had a mouth full of food.

"Just say yes," Adam told him and nudged his arm.

"Yeah, sure." Scott looked at Adam for an explanation.

Dylan rested his hand on Lucas's shoulder and the smile that accompanied the move left Lucas conflicted. The usual warmth and love radiated from Dylan and Lucas's brain stalled. God how he'd love to be wrapped in Dylan's arms right now. No. He couldn't get distracted by thoughts of naked Dylan all hot and sweaty after a session in bed. He needed to talk to Dylan. No sweet smile or strong arms or tight ass beneath equally tight denim would stop him.

"Dylan, can I have a word?" Lucas met his fiancé's eyes. He reached up and squeezed Dylan's hand as he smiled.

Dylan nodded. "Back in a minute, guys."

Lucas guided Dylan to one side. Before he could say anything, Dylan jumped in with, "I couldn't leave him there. If you'd seen the way the kids were treating him…"

Shaking his head, Lucas laughed. "It's not about the dog. The dog can stay." He glanced at the dog and smiled. The animal had its head buried in Scott's crotch, probably sniffing out the many sweet treats the man carried around in his pockets. "It's kind of cute and pathetic looking, and yeah, so long as the two of you keep yourselves out of trouble it'll be fine." He grinned as he turned back to Dylan.

Dylan smiled. "Then what?"

Lucas lowered his eyes and sighed. "There's something I've been meaning to tell you."

"Are you okay? Is it your stomach? We've been doing too much, haven't we? I've been meaning to say something—"

"Dylan, stop," Lucas said. "I'm fine." He pressed his hands to Dylan's chest and enjoyed the feel of the man's strong, solid body beneath his fingertips. He was getting distracted again.

"Okay." Dylan didn't look convinced, but seemed to be going with it.

Why was this so hard? He should just do it before he built this up to something it wasn't. "I wrote to your dad and invited him for Christmas." Reluctantly, he raised his gaze and met Dylan's.

"You did what?" There was a spark of something in the deep ocean blue of Dylan's eyes. He looked alternately horrified then angry. "You do know the minute my mom died that he backed off? That he never once really acknowledged he had a son unless it was to his advantage? You do remember I told you all of this. Right?" His tone implied Lucas was stupid and immediately Lucas felt defensive. He was only doing what he thought best.

"Well, I have Tash and Liam and I just thought—"

Dylan raised his hands as he stepped back. "How could you do that? Go behind my back and ask the man who basically dumped his son on a succession of nannies to come here and spoil my Christmas?" Which did Dylan consider worse? The thought of seeing his father or Lucas's betrayal?

"Christmas is just a day, Dylan—"

"No, it isn't. It's time with people who care about me. I told you I wanted nothing to do with him."

"I just thought…if you and he talked."

Dylan shook his head. "With the man who hasn't had a positive thing to do with my life since he provided the sperm? Well, you thought wrong." Without another word or giving Lucas a chance to explain further, Dylan stormed out of the kitchen.

The kitchen door swung shut. That hadn't gone as well as Lucas had hoped. Something brushed past his leg, and he looked down at the dog who walked up to the door, nudging at it with his nose, clearly wanting to know where his hero had gone. Taking a breath, Lucas turned around and stared across the kitchen. His eyes briefly met Jamie's. All three men looked incredibly uncomfortable as they averted their eyes. He lowered his head and closed his eyes. He was an idiot.

"We'll look after Mutt," Scott said. Lucas opened

his eyes, surprised to find Scott at his side. "Go after him." Scott crouched beside the dog, encouraging the animal to sit.

Lucas nodded. He probably shouldn't let Dylan get too much of a head start. There were plenty of places his lover could seek to hide out. He looked at Scott and said, "Thanks."

## Chapter Four

DYLAN DIDN'T STOP WALKING UNTIL HE GOT AS FAR ON the other side of the Cay as he could. Only when faced with the gently lapping sea on the north of the island did he cease his angry striding. Deflated, he settled down on the sand and stared out at the horizon, his thoughts in turmoil.

He never asked for anyone to contact his dad. He'd explicitly told Lucas on the two occasions they'd talked about Dylan Gray Senior that Dylan wanted nothing to do with the man. They weren't father/son, they were more like distant relatives who had to put up with each other. How did Lucas justify going behind his back like this?

"Dylan?"

Dylan stiffened at his fiancé's voice. Damn this

freaking island for being so frigging small. Could he get no peace at all?

"Go away," he snapped.

"I want to say something."

"You're sorry, okay, now you can fuck off back to the hotel."

Lucas didn't immediately reply, and for a second Dylan thought the other man had gone. Then he heard Lucas sigh and knew he wasn't going to be that lucky. Great, Lucas would want to talk and analyze and list pros and cons. Didn't he realize that sometimes things just *were* and that talking wouldn't fix them?

"I wasn't going to say sorry," Lucas finally said.

Dylan pressed his lips in a tight line to stop his immediate reaction. Sounded about right. Lucas always wanted to be right, with his lists and his considered arguments.

"Leave me alone," Dylan said firmly. "I'm not ready to hear a patented Lucas lecture."

"I don't... I can't..." Lucas clearly had words that weren't in a logical order. That was a first. "I don't lecture," he added lamely. "I try to help."

Dylan stood fast and with intent, and he rounded on Lucas. The guy's expression wasn't mutinous or defensive; the emotions on Lucas's face spoke of uncertainty or sadness. For a second, Dylan stopped but then he pushed past the confusion.

"You don't lecture?" He was incredulous. "What

about the 'settling down on the island speech', or the 'we can't have hot tubs for every cabin' statements."

"We're happily settled here," Lucas defended. "And we don't have the money to throw at unnecessary extra work—"

Dylan didn't let him finish. "I don't want to talk about hot tubs and staying here."

"But you brought them up," Lucas said. He moved so his hands were up in front of him in a defensive posture.

"I reminded you about the times that you think you are the know-it-all genius on this freaking island. I could list so many it would make your head spin."

"I only wrote to him because—"

"I don't want to hear it." Dylan really didn't want to be told why Lucas felt it was right to go behind his back and fuck with his life.

"Dylan, please—"

"I'm serious, Lucas. You can take your concern and shove it where the sun doesn't shine, then you can write back to him and say he's not to step one foot on this island."

"He isn't coming," Lucas said quietly.

Dylan couldn't explain the grip of pain in his chest. Of course his dad wasn't coming. Why the hell would he believe for one minute that Dylan would want to see him?

"So, all you did was make it look like I'd begged

him to visit, and now that he's said no you've made it seem to him like I actually cared."

"Dylan, please—"

"I told you," Dylan shouted. "Go away, Lucas." With that he walked away, in a different direction, to another corner of his little closed-in paradise island. He knew every inch of this place, and there was only one spot he could think of where Lucas wouldn't dare follow to sermonize—the small waterfall and clear spring pond area. As soon as he reached the place, he went to the shack and went through the checklist of what needed doing to this place. The action was familiar and necessary. Concentrating on the shack was important to him and took his thoughts away from the utter desolation he felt that Lucas had betrayed him.

"He's not well," Lucas said simply. "Nothing too serious, but he needed a small operation and can't fly for a few weeks."

Dylan felt a momentary twinge of worry, but he pushed the concern away. Like he actually cared about the man who had so much to say about who and what Dylan was. He didn't answer Lucas either, he couldn't string enough words together, and instead concentrated on checking the upright supports for the small porch. Hurricane season had wreaked its own havoc as it passed through the Cays. This shack was old, and no one could quite explain how it remained standing after each summer, but somehow it survived. The last hurricane had unsettled the shack, pulling a couple of supports inches from the ground. Dylan went to a crouch and pulled away sand from the base of each strut. They would need to fix it.

"Dylan, please, can we talk?"

"Are you still here?" Dylan asked tiredly. "Seriously, go away. You did what you did. I don't want to talk it to death."

"Shout at me, then, punch me, scream at me, but don't walk away." Lucas sat on the small cot-bed mattress that was devoid of bedding. "Please, Dylan. Let me know I haven't completely fucked up."

Dylan cleared away more sand and the repetitive motion was enough to settle his temper a little.

"The one thing," he said in a flat tone. "The only thing I won't talk about and you went behind my back and decided you knew best. So yeah, you fucked up."

"Will you accept my apology?"

"Consider it accepted."

"No."

"What do you mean no?"

"I need you to shout at me, tell me I fucked up, but not in that dead tone. Everything with your dad is inside you, and it's eating away at you. Don't you think Tasha and I would give anything for one more day with our parents? You have a father, but you've cut him dead like he's nothing, and you'll regret it when he's gone." Lucas raised his voice in increments as he talked. He was angry and irritable and Dylan stood in a hurry to face him. Lucas had stood from the cot and his hands were balled into fists and abruptly they were in a faceoff.

"I won't regret a single thing," Dylan said loudly. "He wasn't my dad. He was like a walking bank account who appeared every so often in my life when he absolutely had to."

"He's still your flesh and blood."

"Yeah, that's all he is. When I was eight, he set up a video conference so he could technically attend my birthday party. When I was thirteen, he sent me a check in a card with a twelve on it, and when I was sixteen he gave me a subscription to the *New York Times*. He was waiting for me to bow down and say I'd work with him at his company, futures or some financial shit, and until that moment when we connected with work, he wasn't interested in me. Thing is, we never connected."

"He was grieving as well," Lucas said. "Losing his wife and having a son—"

"Yeah, I get that. He didn't know what to do with a son, not every man is born knowing how to be a father, blah, blah."

"Well, it's true—"

"Don't patronize me," Dylan shouted. He shoved at Lucas's chest and watched in satisfaction when Lucas stumbled back a step. That is what Dylan wanted. Space. Lucas was too close and in and around him—he didn't want Lucas anywhere near him. Dylan's father was a male figure in his life that thought he knew what Dylan wanted. Now he had to add Lucas to that list.

"Babe, I'm not." Lucas held up his hands in a gesture of innocence. "Please. We need to get past this."

"You go back to the hotel. Leave me alone and I'll be home soon. Then we can just ignore this all happened."

Lucas stepped forward and gripped Dylan's arm tight. "No. We're not doing that."

Dylan shook off the hold. "No?" He snorted in disbelief. "I don't think you get a say in this."

"It's what you do," Lucas said with his voice raised again. "We don't talk about your dad, your childhood, yet I see you staring at Tasha and me and I know you enough to see you crave a family connection. But you shut down every time. We need to talk about your dad so we can get past this."

"Or what?" Dylan snapped.

Lucas looked confused. "What do you mean?"

"You gonna leave me if I don't talk to you?"

"Of course not," Lucas said quickly. "I love you. I just want you to be happy."

Dylan stepped closer and poked Lucas in the chest. "I *was* happy until you decided to invite the one person who fucks me over to the only place I have ever had peace in. So, if you can't handle the fact that you overstepped on the only thing guaranteed to destroy you and me, then I don't know why you're still here."

Lucas grabbed Dylan at the upper arms and pulled him in for a brutal kiss. All tongue and teeth, Dylan attempted to pull back until his libido perked up and he realized he was kissing Lucas back just as hard. Why couldn't Lucas see that some things had to remain outside of their relationship? The kiss grew more heated, and Dylan pushed and shoved at Lucas until they were against a wall. This was good, sex with Lucas was always hot and heavy, and sex solved a lot of problems. Temper gave him an edge, and he ground hard against his fiancé and leaned his entire body weight on Lucas so he was pushed back against the old wood with no space to move. He deepened the kiss and tasted blood. When Lucas groaned low in his throat and attempted to push Dylan away, abrupt realization at what he was doing had Dylan releasing the punishing hold and stumbling away.

Lucas's lower lip looked puffy and swollen and blood pearled from a small cut. Shakily, Lucas placed a finger on the cut and looked down at the blood on his hand. He was spaced out, looked shocked, and Dylan's heart broke at that moment.

"Okay," Lucas said. "I get it. I'm sorry for what I did. I'll understand if you... I hope we can..." Then, shaking his head, he pushed past Dylan and left the shack.

Dylan should feel satisfaction. He'd made Lucas see how he felt. Angry and passionate, he had ground his feelings into his lover, and the primitive craving inside him to mark his lover had drawn blood. But it wasn't satisfaction he felt, more like guilt and anguish. Lucas was walking away from him, with blood on his lip and utter defeat in his eyes. Lucas didn't deserve Dylan's anger, he'd just been thinking of Dylan, wanting to help him.

He stumbled out of the shack and caught up with Lucas, and without explanation he spun him around and kissed him again. This time he didn't hold back on the love he felt for this man, and instead of force he used gentle persuasion. With a sigh, Lucas relaxed against him and they kissed lazily and gently for the longest time. When they pulled apart Dylan cradled Lucas's face.

"I'm so sorry," he said. "I didn't mean to hurt you."

"And I'm sorry I tried to fix something that wasn't broken."

Dylan chuckled. "You don't believe that."

"Believe what?"

"You will always think that me and my dad as something to fix."

Lucas had the grace to lower his eyes. When he looked up there was determination in them. "He loves you in his own way," he said. "He said he would have come if he could."

Pain curled in Dylan's chest. The thought of his father sitting and judging everything Dylan had or hadn't done with his life wouldn't exactly have made for a very relaxed Christmas.

"We can agree to disagree, but I promise we'll talk about it."

"I love you," Lucas said gently. "And I am sorry I went behind your back." He didn't add the qualification Dylan expected. There was no buts or ifs.

Emotion welled inside Dylan, and he cupped Lucas's face again. Lucas was so dear to him, the other half of him, the man he wanted to marry. "God, I love you too."

## Chapter Five

LUCAS TOOK DYLAN'S HAND AND WITH THE OTHER HE began to unbutton his fiancé's cutoffs. Awkwardly, he walked toward their spring-fed pool and pulled Dylan with him.

"We need to soak," he said when at first Dylan balked at the pull. Then it seemed he got with the program and soon the two of them were naked and sunk beneath the cool water. There was a natural shelf below the water line, and they sat on the stone and leaned back against the side to stare up at the cloudless blue sky.

"Adam is in his element in the kitchen," Lucas began. He figured if they talked about normal stuff then perhaps he could stop feeling so guilty about what he'd done. He'd written to Dylan Gray Senior with the best of intentions, added to the inherent frustration he had that his fiancé wouldn't talk to him, but at the end of the day he'd handled it badly. Stupid.

"He's good. We need to keep him," Dylan said.

"You think he'll go?"

"Not everyone is a Dominiq. Adam is talented, the same as Scott is with his horticulture. They could have lives elsewhere and be successful."

Lucas nodded. He agreed to a certain extent. At the moment Scott and Adam couldn't keep their hands off each other—still in the honeymoon phase of coming back together. But Dylan was right, and he'd been thinking the same thing.

"I'm thinking we could look at giving Adam a contract. Say, a year, with some decent notice if he decides to move on."

"Agreed."

"And I had this other thought." Lucas paused. This was a potential issue for him and Dylan to disagree on. But with his business head on, he had ideas that would drag Sapphire Cay into a new era.

"Go on…" Dylan encouraged. He pushed off the shelf and turned and treaded water in front of Lucas.

"Shares. A percentage in Sapphire Cay for each year they stay here, something they could buy into, a reward for their work."

Dylan nodded and disappeared under the water for a moment. Lucas had seen him do this before. He could hold his breath for an insanely long time. Enough time at least for Lucas to worry if he was ever coming up for air. When he finally appeared, he smoothed his long hair back from his face and his beautiful ocean-blue eyes sparkled with enthusiasm.

"That is a really cool idea. Like a profit-sharing thing."

Lucas didn't correct Dylan's summing up and instead smiled. "They could end up having a real stake, make a life here."

Dylan chuckled. "Then we could rename ourselves Gay Cay."

"Ass." But there was no heat in his words. He shuffled on his seat as Dylan moved to straddle his lap.

"I'm so sorry I hurt you," Dylan whispered. He gently kissed the split in Lucas's lip, and Lucas linked his hands behind Dylan's neck to deepen the kiss. He craved this, wanted the kiss so bad. Dylan backed away, and Lucas smiled as he chased for more.

"He was never there when I needed him to be," Dylan said gently.

"Your dad."

"Yeah. All the times when a boy needs his dad or his mom, he wasn't there. He was in China or England or wherever the hell his work took him. He was grieving about Mom, he was focused on giving me a good life, and I know that. I listen to you as you tell me your parents died and jeez, I don't know how you managed to hold it together or sacrifice what you did to bring up Tasha. I understand I'm lucky to have a parent still alive, I just can't reconcile the facts with what I feel inside me. So, can we leave it a few days? Because I never realized how much shit I have in my head that needs sorting out."

"I never meant to upset you," Lucas said. He listened to Dylan talk, and he felt like he'd been the one to take the lid off the can of worms. He'd done it because he'd cared, because he'd seen Dylan's introspection when he and Tasha hugged. But he'd never meant to hurt Dylan, even though he knew Dylan wouldn't be happy.

"Guess you could owe me," Dylan said with another kiss.

"Owe you how?" Like Lucas didn't know what Dylan was going to say.

"One of your massages with the oil, maybe?" Dylan suggested, this time with a grin.

"I can do that."

"First off though, I'm thinking we're naked in the pool and we need to take advantage of every minute alone we get this holiday."

"Considering Edward wants to organize us, I think that is a good idea."

"So, you're naked, I'm naked, I'm hard…" He

pressed down into Lucas' lap. "Seems you're hard as well. Shame to waste it."

Lucas chuckled into another kiss. They had nothing here, no lube, but they had hands and lips and hell, just kissing Dylan was enough to get him close to the edge. They hugged and teased, and slippery-slow they ground against each other.

When Dylan came he buried his face in Lucas's neck. "I love you," he said.

Lucas followed soon after and his *I love you* was so heartfelt that his voice hitched with emotion. Dylan kissed him and they sat this way, with the sun high in the sky and the water cool around them, as they relaxed in the aftermath. Lucas could sleep here with Dylan in his arms, if only he could trust that they wouldn't float away and drown.

Finally, he squeezed Dylan's arms. "We need to move out of here," he said.

"Mmmm," Dylan replied sleepily.

"You are not falling asleep on me," Lucas warned. "Let's go and sit in the shack."

They clambered out and pulled on shorts and tees. Lucas couldn't stop the stupid grin he knew he had on his face. Good thing Dylan had a similar grin, otherwise Lucas could have looked ridiculous.

Hand in hand they walked back to the shack, but they didn't climb on the cot to cuddle. Instead, Dylan fell to his knees next to the raised strut and examined it closely. "It's like the sand dislodged and the hurricane sucked up at the supports."

"Can we save it?"

"It's stood for God knows how many years, I'm thinking a bit of attention and we can make sure it's fine for a few more. Support the weight and I'll have a better look."

Lucas supported the weight of the strut and pushed a little so that it lifted some more. Dylan dug deeper to find out what they needed to do to save the structure. This was their quiet space, along with the waterfall, and Lucas wasn't ready for anything, not even hurricanes, to destroy their place.

"There's something stuck here," Dylan said. He grunted with exertion as he pulled at whatever was lodged under the strut.

"Is it a root or something?" Lucas asked. He couldn't see a thing from where he was standing.

"A metal something," Dylan replied. "I'm just getting my hand behind...it's a box...a tin box... hang on..."

"Hanging," Lucas said with a smile.

Finally, Dylan sat back on his ass in the sand. In his hands he had an old cookie tin type of box. Placing it on the ground, he picked up a handful of stones and a larger rock and refilled the hole.

"Okay, I think you can let go of the upright."

Carefully, Lucas let go but held his hands near in case the whole thing collapsed around them. When the strut sat firmly in the stones and he was happy it wasn't moving, he stepped back and away. Dylan sat next to the tin and pulled it onto his lap.

"What if it's buried treasure?" Lucas said with a smirk. "Gold doubloons."

"In a cookie tin that looks like it's from before we were even born?"

"I was joking, ass," Lucas said. "It looks like the old stuff from before World War Two. Open it."

Dylan ran a finger on the embossed surface of the tin and hesitated. "What if it's empty."

"Is it heavy?"

Dylan lifted it and shook it. Something rattled inside. He tried to open it, but it was sealed so tightly because it was warped in shape that he couldn't at first get into it. Finally, he used the edge of a key to prize it open and Lucas peered in as soon as the lid was off.

Letters, shells, a stone, and a gold chain with an anchor on the end of it. The letters were bundled together and tied with a pale-colored ribbon.

"Someone's memories," he murmured softly.

"This feels kind of wrong," Dylan said reverently. He picked up the chain and it dangled from his finger. Tarnished, it hung there and the anchor spun in his hold. "This belonged to someone."

"Alfie," Lucas said. He pointed to the letters. "That one is addressed to Alfie."

"A conch shell," Dylan said, "and a few other shells I don't know." He pushed them aside. Under the letters were photos wrapped in material. Some of the pictures were gone, nothing more that speckles on paper, but others remained unharmed. He handed them to Lucas, who carefully picked his way through. Then he saw something that made him stop and stare.

"Look." He held out the photo he found. Dylan looked at it and his mouth fell open.

Two men naked and laughing, staring at the camera, arms wrapped around each other, sat on the edge of Dylan and Lucas's pool.

"Wow," Dylan summed up. "Who do you think they are?"

"Whoever they were, if this was Alfie, and what, a friend, they were happy."

Dylan smiled. "I don't think they were just friends," he said. "Look at the love in that photo." He pointed to the next photo down. One of the men was looking directly into the camera, his mouth curved in a smile and one hand in his dark hair.

"That's stunning," Lucas said softly. He turned the photo over. *Alfie, 1935, Sapphire Cay*. Under the words was a small heart and the initials *AJ* and *PF*, with the simple word, *forever* added. "So that is Alfie," Lucas said. "I wonder if the other guy is the PF. I wonder what the J stands for in AJ?"

"Shall we take it back to the hotel? It feels weird opening it here." Dylan nodded toward the pool and waterfall.

Lucas couldn't agree more. "Yeah."

Scooping the contents back in the box, Dylan held it under his arm, and hand in hand they walked back to the hotel. They heard the voices before they saw who was talking, although it was obviously Edward with Jamie calming him down.

"Dog shit, Jamie. Why me?"

"Stop walking it around." Jamie was laughing.

"My Ferragamos! Do you know how much these cost? Don't laugh. I hate you, Jamie Antoine Durand."

Lucas grimaced and he and Dylan exchanged glances as they walked out to where Edward was standing on one foot and Jamie was near purple in the face from laughing. Of all the people to step in Mutt's deposits, it had to be Edward.

The two of them turned to face Lucas and Dylan. Edward slipped off a shoe and waggled it in front of Dylan's face.

"Explain," he ordered.

Just the look on the wedding planner's face—horror, shock, disgust—plus Jamie laughing, and Lucas couldn't help himself. He began to snort in laughter, and when Dylan joined in, Edward couldn't stop the faint smile on his lips.

"I hate you all," he said without heat. "I'm going in to find someone who appreciates good shoes."

Lucas thought of Adam or Scott, or even Tasha and Liam, and laughed even harder.

No one appreciated shoes like Edward did.

No one.

## Chapter Six

EDWARD ROLLED OVER IN BED AND DRAPED HIS ARM across Jamie's waist. A faint smile curled the corner of his mouth as he spooned against his boyfriend's back. With a sigh, he tucked the bed sheet between them. Jamie was always so damn hot, and many a night Edward had woken stuck to his lover in an uncomfortable damp heat. Breathing in deeply, Edward tried to get comfortable. He needed to get up. There was still a list as long as his arm to sort through before the Croft's New Year wedding. But he'd promised Jamie he'd stop for a few days and enjoy Christmas on the island and then the couple of days back in Miami with Jamie's parents.

They'd been together for just over a year and Jamie had decided it was time Edward started getting involved in Durand family events. Edward didn't really see what the issue was. He'd worked with Jamie's parents for years and didn't understand what Jamie's obsession was with instigating further bonding situations. A family dinner here and there seemed enough to him. He'd met Jamie's sister and the kids. He'd even attended Jamie's grandmother's ninetieth birthday party. The old dear had a mean grip, a wicked sense of humor, and loved her grandson fiercely. Edward had been warned not to break Jamie's heart. It had been easy for him to agree not to.

Opening his eyes, Edward stared at the back of Jamie's head. His gaze fell to the chain around Jamie's neck below the line of his hair. He loved Jamie. He loved the man for who he was, who he used to be, and was more certain than ever about sticking around to see who Jamie was yet to become. Jamie had a solid job with Bowyer Industries and had been offered promotion from intern to permanent staff. Between that and joining Edward on and off on Sapphire Cay, things were going great for the former Marine. Hell, everything was fantastic for both of them.

Jamie stirred and rolled over. A sleepy smile crossed his lips as he slowly opened his eyes. Looking through his lashes, Jamie settled his gaze on Edward's mouth before moving in for a kiss. "Morning," he said and stretched his arms above his head. He yawned. "What time is it?"

"I have no idea," Edward said. Taking advantage of Jamie raising his arms, Edward shuffled forward and rested his head on Jamie's chest. Gently, he ran his fingers over the raised scars across his lover's skin. "And I don't care."

Jamie laughed. "First time for everything," he said. Jamie knew better than anyone how regimented Edward's days could be. Edward wrote everything in his planner, an hour by hour breakdown of every phone call he needed to make, appointment he had to keep, and delivery he had scheduled. "Did you enjoy yourself last night?"

Heat spread through Edward's chest and downward as he recalled the evening. Lucas had organized a barbeque on the patio, and after much wine, grilled meat, and laughs, Jamie had stolen Edward away to the staff quarters. They had barely made it through the door to their cabin before Jamie stripped down to the waist and manhandled Edward across the room and onto the bed.

"I did," Edward finally said. The memory shot to the head of his dick. In one quick move, he straddled Jamie's hips. The manoeuver left Edward a little lightheaded, but the feel of Jamie equally hard beneath him and pressing into his left ass cheek helped him regain his focus.

"What are you doing?" Jamie asked sleepily.

Grinning, Edward leaned forward as he pressed Jamie's hands into the pillow on either side of his head.

He wriggled his ass and smiled as Jamie groaned at the forced friction.

"I thought you were sleepy—"

Edward shut Jamie up with a kiss. Gently, he rubbed his nose against Jamie's and slid his hands along the length of Jamie's arms to cup his face. Passionately, he kissed him again, all the time rotating his body as he teased Jamie's erection. Edward closed his eyes as Jamie reached up and ran his fingers through his hair. He breathed in deeply and enjoyed the delicious chill that crept over his skin at Jamie's soft touches. Jamie could touch and ruffle Edward's hair as much as he liked. Their bed was the one place Edward had learned to let go.

"What do you want to do today?" Jamie asked. He glided his fingers through Edward's hair and across his face, neck, and shoulders.

Edward opened his eyes and wrapped his hands around Jamie's. Slowly, he kissed each of Jamie's fingers before teasingly sucking his lover's index finger. "I can think of one thing."

A smile spread across Jamie's face, and before Edward realized what was happening, Jamie had him in his arms and had rolled him onto his back. Jamie moved between his legs and pressed their erections together as he roamed his hands over Edward's skin. Jamie moved quickly, and positioning himself just right, he began to rub his body against Edward.

"Oh God," Edward said. He wanted Jamie in him all over again. Just the thought of sex with the Marine was enough to make his whole body tingle in anticipation. Jamie was an incredible lover and he seemed to know exactly how and where to touch Edward to draw out soft whimpers and full primal growls.

"Fuck me," Edward whispered at Jamie's ear as he nipped Jamie's earlobe.

"Again?" Jamie said, though it was clear from his heaving chest and heated skin he was already there and wanted Edward as much as Edward wanted him.

"Uh-huh," Edward managed. He squeezed his thighs against Jamie's waist. "We're on vacation, right?" Jamie had given him the hard sell plenty of times already, telling Edward to put the planner down and just go with it, whatever the hell *it* was.

Jamie kissed Edward on the mouth and lingered there in a series of teasing licks and nips. He skimmed his hands over Edward's skin and stroked the inside of Edward's thigh. From the look in his eyes, Jamie needed no further words from Edward to convince him Christmas Eve morning was clearly the best time for another lovemaking session.

"I love you," Jamie said.

Edward smiled and kissed Jamie again. "I love you, too." Edward drew his lip between his teeth at the delicious feel of Jamie wrapping his hand around his cock. Jamie's grip was firm and his gentle teasing turned into a steady rhythm as he stroked Edward's erection. Edward closed his eyes and twisted his fingers in the bed sheets. With his other hand, Jamie had cupped Edward's balls, massaging them, and with each stroke of Edward's dick, he slid his finger toward Edward's hole, teasing the outer ring of muscle just right.

Pulling Jamie close, Edward smothered him in kisses. He wanted Jamie in him, filling him with his thick dick and fucking him to ecstasy. "In. Now."

Quickly, Jamie coated his dick in lube and then leaned over Edward. Carefully, he pressed forward, nipping his lower lip as he sank into Edward with ease. "Shit, I must have fucked you good last night."

"You certainly made an impression," Edward teased. He groaned slightly and welcomed the return to fullness as Jamie leaned in close, his thighs flush with Edward's ass. Holding onto Jamie's shoulders, Edward made slow movements, creating waves against Jamie's cock. "Fuck me already, soldier." He smiled knowingly as Jamie quirked an eyebrow. Jamie grinned and thrust his hips over and over, eliciting a small cry from Edward.

"Marine," Edward corrected himself on a whisper and met Jamie's eyes. "Marine."

Jamie kissed him as he set a pace. Thrust after thrust, he somehow managed to ignite every nerve inside Edward, bringing them both to climax in a torrid of excited words and sounds. Spent, Jamie fell forward and rested on Edward's chest. "You make me so fucking horny," he said. He kissed a line between Edward's nipples and blew his breath across the nub he'd teased to attention.

"Good to know," Edward said. He stroked his hands through Jamie's dark hair, gently separating it into three strands.

"Don't you dare," Jamie mumbled against Edward's chest.

"What?" Edward said. He chuckled to himself as he started plaiting the longest of the strands.

Jamie lifted his head and rested his chin on Edward's chest. "You're such an ass."

"Good job you love me, then." He tugged Jamie's hair. "Now shut up and let me make you look all pretty."

SITTING ON THE END OF THE BED, EDWARD SLOWLY RAN his hands over his silk tie. He gently touched his brow and smoothed back his hair. Jamie had convinced him to lose the hair products for the day. To say he felt naked was an overstatement, granted, but he did feel a smidge underdressed.

"You look fine," Jamie said from behind him.

Looking over his shoulder, Edward's gaze settled on Jamie still naked and spread out on the bed. That was how he felt right now. Jamie was the only one to see him out of his Edward-the-wedding-planner garb.

"Thanks," he said. He took a deep breath and stared toward the door to the cabin.

The ruffle of sheets and the dip of the mattress were quickly followed by Jamie wrapping his arms around Edward's waist. "Are you okay? You just seem...sad."

"I was thinking about Andrew and Emily and my parents."

Jamie kissed Edward's shoulder through the material of his shirt. "About being home with them?"

Edward shrugged. His brother still lived at home; he had their parents for support. "Not like I'd be much use." Emily had moved in with Andrew into the converted garage of his and Andrew's parents' home. Things had moved on from there, an engagement and then the announcement Emily was pregnant. Barely seven days after their twelve-week scan, Emily lost the baby. The couple had only made the news public after the scan, when everything with the baby had seemed fine and healthy. But just as quickly they had to make a new announcement, their joy ripped from them.

"These things happen. It's nobody's fault and they understand you have your life over here," Jamie said supportively.

"I know," Edward said. "But my brother was so excited about becoming a dad, and my parents, they couldn't wait to be grandparents."

"And you'd have been an uncle."

"Yeah. Yeah I would." Edward gave a small smile. "Still might. I'm sure they'll try again."

Jamie rested his chin on Edward's shoulder and kissed his cheek. "How about in the New Year we see about taking a vacation? We could go over to England and I could meet everybody."

Pursing his lips, Edward considered the idea. He had so much he needed to do in the next few months and had weddings booked through to the following March. "You know how early people book weddings. I'm already planning things eighteen months ahead."

"I know, and I'm not talking about taking weeks," Jamie persisted. "Plus, you've been looking to get Marylou-Beth doing more. Making her more a partner than just the hired help. Maybe it could be a trial run."

"And who would be her PA?" Edward asked. "I don't have time to be running interviews and showing newbies the ropes." He sounded snippy and what had been a relaxing morning now had him agitated.

"Marylou, she could interview. She knows how you and Blush Pink work. She's not stupid."

Edward quickly did the math. If Marylou-Beth moved up to planner, he would need two new PAs. He hadn't planned for it to be this soon, but he didn't see any issues financially. "I'll think about it," he said. He could pick a week without an actual wedding, leave Marylou-Beth with orders and meetings and the like.

"That's all I asked," Jamie assured him.

"Okay," Edward said. He pressed his mouth to Jamie's and gently cupped the man's face. It would be nice to see his family, not just voices on the end of the phone or words in an email. Breathing in deeply, Edward then got to his feet and smoothed the lines of his clothes. The action was comforting and helped free him from his malaise. Feeling more like himself, he looked at Jamie and then clapped his hands together. "Chop chop. We have a tree to help decorate."

Jamie laughed and fell back against the mattress. "Slave driver."

Edward grabbed Jamie by his ankles and gently tugged at his legs. Meeting Jamie's beautiful green eyes, he said, "You wouldn't have me any other way."

## Chapter Seven

"WHAT YOU UP TO?" DYLAN PEERED OVER AT THE PILES of paperwork on Lucas's desk. Some was on yellow paper, some on white. Dylan knew enough that the yellow was accounts information, the white held booking details.

"Just matching bookings to invoices," Lucas answered in that patient explanatory tone he never failed to use when Dylan ever showed an interest in the office.

"Can I help?"

Lucas looked up at him with a comical look of horror on his face. "No," he said quickly. Dylan chuckled. As much as his fiancé had relaxed here on the Cay, he was still all about taking control when it came to paperwork.

"I could staple stuff," Dylan teased. He leaned over

to grab the stapler, but before he could reach it, Lucas picked it up and held it to his chest.

"Don't you have a dog to walk?" Lucas asked.

"Mutt's asleep outside on the gazebo." Dylan gave a wry smile at the name Scott had given to the dog yesterday. For some reason it had stuck. Not that anyone would argue, considering the drowned rat impression Scott had pulled off after his attempt to bath the dog.

"Did you—"

"Yes. I made a collar out of one of your belts and fastened it to a long length of rope. He's fine."

"My belt?"

Dylan shrugged. "You know I don't have a single belt to my name, and I didn't think I could handle Edward crying if I used one of his."

Lucas nodded. "Good call."

"So…when are you finished?" Dylan was aware he was slightly leaning toward whining, but this was Christmas Eve, they had no guests, and he wanted Lucas time.

"The sooner you go annoy someone else, the sooner I'll be done," Lucas said with a smile.

"Can I at least get a kiss?"

Lucas sighed noisily, but he didn't hesitate to get behind the kiss. Dylan used every trick in the book from the way he slid his tongue against Lucas to the tiny path of bites he nibbled from lips to chin. When he pulled back, Lucas near stumbled over the desk to chase for the kiss and Dylan chuckled.

Lucas shook his head. "You're a child. You know that, right?"

Dylan grinned at him, then lifted the laptop and the cookie tin they'd found off his messy desk—he didn't spend a long time in here, that was more Lucas's domain, but still he managed to collect paperwork and folders. "I'm going to research what we found yesterday."

"Good luck finding anything," Lucas replied, distracted. He'd sat down and begun pulling individual yellow sheets from the main pile.

"Thought I could phone Antoine and Jeanie, see if they know any stories. I may try Jamie first, though, see what he may have heard." Antoine and Jeanie were Jamie's parents, and the two of them had been the owners of the Cay for over thirty years before selling to Dylan. "And Dominiq," he added. Lucas wasn't listening. He was frowning and tapping away at a calculator, and as quietly as he could, Dylan left the room. Knowing Lucas, he'd be in the office for a couple of hours, and Dylan decided he'd find coffee, then a quiet corner where he could concentrate.

The kitchen was empty. They'd decided as a group that they could all handle their own breakfasts over Christmas, which gave Adam a break. He rummaged for bread and made toast, then waited patiently for the coffee machine to do its thing.

"Morning," Tasha said from behind him. Dylan turned to face his sister-in-law-in-all-but-name with a ready grin on his face. He loved her to bits and had a big space for her in his heart. His grin dropped when he saw how pale she looked.

"Are you okay?" he asked quickly. Putting his plate down, he stepped to her side and placed a hand on her forehead. She didn't seem like she was running a fever.

She smiled at the attention. "I'm just tired and I didn't sleep so well."

"Is there a problem? With the bed or something?" Dylan pulled her in for a hug. He heard her soft laugh as she buried her face against him.

"Too quiet," she said. "No cars or sirens or neighbors." She moved back and away.

"Exactly what Lucas used to say."

"By tomorrow I'll be used to it and sleep will be easy."

"Can I get you some coffee?"

"Nothing for me. Some toast, maybe?"

Dylan immediately handed her his plate with the two slices of toast. "Have mine, I'll make some more."

"Sure?"

"Sure."

Tasha reached up and kissed his cheek. "You're a

good man, Dylan." Then with a sketched wave, Tasha and the toast left the room. He considered whether or not to bother with toast and instead piled a bowl with fresh fruit and one of yesterday's cookie batch. That would do.

With coffee, fruit, cookie, tin, and laptop, he went out to the gazebo and settled himself at one of the small tables to one side and in the shade. At this distance from the main house, they could get internet if they were lucky. He started his laptop, and while eating the bowl of fruit he turned his attention to the box of stuff they'd found. Digging out his cell, he photographed each individual item and bemoaned the fact that at least ten of the photos were beyond repair. Water damage, maybe? Or quality of processing? Either way he piled those to one side and concentrated on the photos that remained clear.

Then he opened a Word document and began typing in notes. He began with the initials AJ and PF, filling in Alfie for a Christian name. Then he emailed from his cell to the laptop and began collating the photos with the information. Something stopped him from reading the letters, so they remained in the bundle with the pale ribbon. The fact that a few of the photos held images of the guy, Alfie, naked—and one in graphic detail had the two men embracing and nude—made Dylan think he was looking at a homosexual liaison. The faint stamp on the top letter was December 1943, the earliest 1935.

Eight years of letters then nothing. Just a box buried in the sand.

*I wonder if their forever was like my forever with Lucas?* Or was it hidden? Cut short by war?

His laptop finally connected to the internet, and before it could change its damn mind, Dylan entered in random snippets of information to see what he could find. Sapphire Cay had a few entries, the most notable of which—besides the information linking to the resort itself—was one particular entry. A throwaway line that Google listed on page seven of the searches.

"Peter French to wed Annalisa Bainbridge" was the title of the post and the search words that came up underneath were the words *wedding* and *Sapphire Cay*. Dylan clicked on the link, then may as well have gone for a nap for the amount of time it took the internet to deliver a result. Meanwhile, he held the gold chain up to the light and buffed at it with the hem of his T-shirt. There was an inscription on the back, and he peered at it closely.

Damn his eyes, but the engraving was way too small. He needed Edward and his freaky-assed glasses that could read even the tiniest of print. Glancing back at the screen, he read from the top. The page was a Wikipedia entry about the French Foundation. With roots going back to the early 1900s, it appeared the Foundation had fingers in an awful lot of pies. Frederick French, the founder, was apparently influential with

Presidents and CEOs alike. His son Peter, born 1915 and the heir to the whole mansion-and-huge-inheritance thing, was listed as having died in 1994, aged seventy-nine. He had no heirs, although he'd been married to Annalisa Bainbridge of the New York Bainbridges—whoever they were—for five years from 1937.

The Foundation was charity-run now, and there were links to resources Dylan could check up on when he was back in the office.

"Morning," Jamie called over as he and Edward strolled hand in hand from the cabins and up past the back of the house. Edward hadn't bothered gelling his hair this morning, and it fell in loose layers to the bottom of his ears in length. He looked different, less uptight, although that only lasted until he spotted Mutt on the gazebo.

"If he shits on my gazebo…" Edward warned. Mutt had obviously taken a shine to Edward and Jamie and bounded over toward them, the length of the rope stopping him a few inches short. Jamie immediately went to his knees to fuss Mutt, but Edward circled the two of them with apprehension on his face. Finally, he stood by the table, and with a huff, he slumped into the seat next to Dylan.

"I know he's your dog…" he began.

"I know. I know. Clean up after him and don't let him anywhere near guests. I've already got the pre-approved Lucas rules."

"Is he staying?" Jamie called from his prone position with Mutt climbing all over him.

"Lucas put a call in to the mainland to report we had him, but I'm convinced he is a stray that needs a home."

Jamie finally pushed himself up to stand and made to kiss Edward. Dylan had to laugh when Edward reared back in horror.

"Dog smell." He shuddered. Jamie joined in the laughing, and Edward, looking horrified, didn't last very long before he had a grin on his face as well.

"What's that?" Jamie asked curiously. He picked up a photo and peered at the watermarked image. "You really need new porn," he joked.

"They're not porn," Dylan snapped quickly. He didn't like the comment, and he pinned his instant annoyance on the fact that these weren't porn of any sort, but images of love. He held out his hand.

Jamie placed the photo carefully back into Dylan's care. "Okay," he said while looking confused.

"Sorry. Just...we found a box by the shack, lifted loose in the last hurricane, and it had letters and photos in it."

"Really? Bloody hell," Edward said. He'd never sounded so British as he did then. "Did you read the letters?"

Dylan shook his head. "It doesn't feel right. I'm just trying to piece together some of the information from the photos. Initials and dates, that kind of thing. PF is, I think, Peter French."

"Is he the guy in the photos?"

"In the double shots possibly. But the guy on his own..." Dylan rummaged until he found the shot of Alfie with the date. "This guy is named Alfie, and we think his surname is something starting with a J. Don't suppose you know anything about an Alfie? Or Peter French? Or Annalisa Bainbridge? Possibly a wedding on the Cay here? Would have been just before the time World War Two started."

Jamie shook his head. "Nothing I recall," he said. "I could ask Mom and Dad."

"Thanks. That was my next stop. I think I have as much information as I can without reading the letters, and I'm not ready to do that yet, nor is Lucas."

"Morning." This time it was from Scott, who was bleary eyed and yawning as he dropped onto the steps of the gazebo.

"Did someone keep you up?"

"Like you wouldn't believe," Scott said on another yawn. "Only it wasn't for the good stuff. Adam kept talking in his sleep about turkeys and gravy and whether he could find a recipe for seaweed sauce."

Jamie snorted a laugh that set everyone off. "Adam's taking Christmas Dinner seriously, then," he pointed out.

"Christmas Day, seven pm, the dining room, and I

swear, if he serves seaweed sauce with the turkey, I'll cause a distraction while you all hide it."

"What seaweed sauce?" Adam asked from the main door. He looked significantly more awake than Scott.

"The one you're giving us for dinner tomorrow," Scott said. Adam sat next to his partner on the step and frowned as he leaned against him.

"And I say again, what seaweed sauce?"

"You spent most of the night talking in your sleep about it," Scott explained. "That and snowflake fritters, whatever the hell they are."

Adam bit his lip. "Should I apologize?" he asked softly. Dylan sometimes caught that fleeting spark of insecurity in the younger man's tone, but Scott dealt with it in his usual inimitable manner. He grabbed Adam in a bear hug, then kissed him soundly.

"You should hear what Edward talks about in his sleep. Last night he was telling me we needed real fairies on the tree," Jamie said.

Edward bristled. "I am clearly the only one taking the decorating of the tree seriously."

Dylan took his cue and tidied up the box contents, and carrying them, the empty fruit bowl, and the laptop, he walked inside to prize Lucas away from the office. He left to the noise of Jamie announcing he was walking Mutt, Edward arguing with him, and Scott and Adam teasing each other about seaweed sauce.

It was good to hear the chaos and know everyone here was happy.

When he got to the office, Lucas was shutting down the computer and didn't argue when Dylan suggested that was the last of what needed doing until after Christmas.

"Time for Christmas," Dylan said.

Lucas smiled. "So, what first?"

# Chapter Eight

*DON'T SAY ANYTHING*. JAMIE TUGGED AT THE SLEEVE OF Edward's shirt in an attempt to hold him back. He could see the man itching to attack the tree and rearrange the garlands and decorations into his usual style of perfection.

The group had met in the guest lounge in order to decorate the nine-foot Christmas tree. Edward had insisted on them getting a real tree brought over to the island, one that apparently wouldn't be leaving needles everywhere and smelled bloody good. Jamie pressed his lips in a line. He'd been around Edward far too long.

"Remember these?" Tasha said. She held two sewn-felt tree ornaments out to Lucas.

Jamie strained to see what they were.

"You kept these?" Lucas sounded amazed. He held the pair of what Jamie realized were miniature stockings up for the rest of the group to see. "We stitched them ourselves."

"You don't say?" Edward said softly, though Jamie recognized the Brit's usual sarcasm bubbling below the surface.

"Well, you did yours. I got help from Mom," Tasha said with a laugh. "Hence mine looks so amazing." She grinned and looked at Edward. "Think they might catch on?"

Edward seemed to soften at the mention of Lucas and Tasha's mother. He smiled and shrugged. "They're very homely," he said. "If that's what you like."

Jamie could only imagine how hard it was for Edward to watch the disorder to the way the tree was being decorated—tinsel thrown onto the branches unevenly, no sense, symmetry, or color scheme to how the ornaments were being hung.

"Left," Edward whispered as Tasha and Lucas each hung one of the stockings on the tree. He clicked his tongue as he scratched behind his ear. Jamie looked at the tree, and sure enough on the left there was a space that needed filling. Stepping forward, Jamie eyed the remaining baubles and picked one up. It was a pale shade of green covered in glitter. Brown stained the bauble—old glue where glitter had rubbed away. He zoned in on the bare section of the tree and hung the bauble perfectly. Turning around, he met Edward's eyes. Edward raised an eyebrow and smiled, seemingly glad that at least one person in the room got him and the art of decorating.

"That was an ugly bauble," Edward said as Jamie rejoined him.

"Sure was," Jamie said. He couldn't help but smile as he felt Edward's hand in his. "You want to do one?"

Edward had stayed away from the tree so far. He hadn't seemed keen to contribute to the atrocity being created before them. "I'm fine," Edward said.

"Here," Scott said.

Jamie stared at his hands as Scott handed him a spray can of fake snow.

"These, too." Scott handed a packet of stencils to Edward.

Edward looked like he'd just caught a whiff of dog shit. "Erm, I don't think so." He held his hands in a 'can't you see I'm wearing Gucci' pose.

"Just crack a window. You'll be fine."

Edward went to complain, but Scott used his tried-and-tested Edward response of walking away before becoming embroiled in an argument he'd never win. Edward didn't lose arguments. Ever.

"Come on," Jamie said. "It'll be fun." He walked toward the dining room and Edward followed.

"Fun? You won't be the one stressing about it when the Crofts want their crystal-clear ocean view from the dining room. This stuff is horrible to get off windows. I can imagine Scott's halfhearted cleaning and all the filthy smears we'll come back to."

Jamie stopped, turned around, and pulled Edward into a kiss. "Shut up," he said. Edward simply opened his mouth and immediately closed it, seemingly lost for words for a change. "Lucas promised to have this place a blank canvas for your return. Have a little faith."

"More likely I'll need a Christmas miracle," Edward said. He lowered his head as a smile cracked his face.

"Better?"

The snap of wit had somehow reset Edward back to factory settings. "Yes." He held up the stencils and pointed at the first one. "What is this even supposed to be?"

Jamie leaned close. "A train driven by a bear I think."

Turning around the pack, Edward eyed the image. "So it is. Silly me." He shot Jamie a less-than-convinced look.

Jamie snatched the stencils from Edward and walked over to the patio doors at the back of the dining room. Pulling out the stencils, he sorted through them to find some of the better images. "Come and hold this," he said, waving Edward over. He held a stencil of a present up to the window and waited as Edward reluctantly joined him. "Now stay still." He shook the can of snow and pulled off the lid.

"Don't get any on me," Edward insisted. He awkwardly held the stencil by the corners.

"Don't be such a baby. I know exactly what I'm doing."

"WANKER!" EDWARD SNAPPED.

Jamie stood in the doorway between the lounge and dining room and winced as Edward slammed the door opposite closed. Six pairs of eyes stared at him and Jamie felt somewhat awkward.

"Now what did you do?" Scott asked.

"I may have got some of the spray-on snow on Edward's sleeves." Together with his ruined shoes from yesterday, Edward had finally boiled over from being slightly-irritated-but-okay-because-it-was-kind-of-amusing to oh-hell-no.

"Isn't that a Hugo Boss shirt?" Adam asked. "They're like one hundred dollars a pop." Jamie felt a twinge of jealousy that the ex-con seemed to understand the gravitas of the situation beyond what he himself could. To him it was just a shirt.

Scott rested his hand on his lover's shoulders and was clearly having some sort of moment of pride. "You should probably go get him," Scott told Jamie. "Apologize and shit."

"Tell him lunch is nearly ready." Adam got to his feet. The man had been in and out of the kitchen for the last forty minutes checking on the various buffet bits he had in the oven. "Just need Scott to come help plate them up and then we're ready."

Handing the stencils to Dylan to finish, he headed out in pursuit of Edward. When Jamie eventually found Edward, he was surprised to find him sitting on the steps to the gazebo, Mutt at his feet as he stroked the dog's coat.

"Hey," Jamie said. He sat on the step beside Edward and joined in the petting of the dog. With a bit of grooming and a bath, Mutt already looked a hell of a lot better. "I'm sorry about your shirt."

Edward pursed his mouth in a thoughtful pout. "I overreacted. I know that."

"Then why are you sitting out here?"

"Because I'd already stormed out. I felt stupid enough without coming straight back in."

Jamie laughed and quickly pulled Edward into a hug. "You're an idiot," Jamie said softly.

Edward hugged Jamie back. "When I look at you, I do wonder sometimes."

"Ass," Jamie said. "You know getting with me was the smartest thing you ever did." He closed his eyes and held Edward close. He loved the feel of the man in his arms, the way Edward smelled, and the taste of his kisses. He held Edward's face and kissed him, enjoying the affection that radiated from his lover. "You coming back inside?" He released Edward and smiled as Mutt playfully bounded up the gazebo steps and half climbed on his back as the dog tried to lick his face.

"You'll be covered in dog hair," Edward said, leaning back to avoid the romping animal. He met Jamie's eyes and must have noted the mischief in them. "Oh, don't you even think of it." He shuffled sideways and yelped as Jamie pounced on him, followed by Mutt. The three of them tumbled from the steps to the ground. Jamie straddled Edward's legs and tickled him, Mutt bounced with excitement, and Edward laughed, seemingly no longer caring about his shoes, his shirt, or the fact he was lying on the grass.

Jamie stopped, rolled off Edward, and lay breathlessly on the ground beside him. He reached out and took Edward's hand as they both looked up at the clear blue sky.

"Maybe September," Edward finally said.

"September?" Jamie asked.

"You wanted to see the UK, right? My family? We could go for September. See my folks and my brother in Devon and then maybe travel around for a couple of weeks."

"The whole month?" Jamie said surprised.

Edward turned his head. He seemed to settle his gaze on Jamie's mouth. Jamie was proved right when Edward leaned in and kissed him. "The Cay's closed 'til the end of October. I only have one wedding that month, and like you said, Marylou-Beth knows exactly how I work and how I'd do things. I think she could handle it."

Jamie smiled and leaned forward. His turn to kiss Edward. "I'd like that."

"We could rediscover my roots together. Exeter, Torquay, Plymouth. Crazy golf on the seafront. Oh and chips. Real chips in polystyrene boxes with battered fish and mushy peas." Edward smiled. "Amusement arcades. I used to spend hours feeding coppers into the penny pushers." He met Jamie's eyes. "Sorry."

"I'd love to see where you grew up," Jamie said. He'd never been to the UK, but since meeting Edward, he was interested to see what the nation was like—and not just from the stereotypes he'd seen on the TV. Though he did admit to having a thing for English bad guys portrayed in movies. He wouldn't kick Tom Hardy or Tom Hiddleston out of bed, that was for sure.

They stayed on the ground for a moment until Mutt decided it was time for them to move. Mutt pushed at Jamie's stomach with his front paws, encouraging him to sit up and pay the dog some attention. Jamie ruffled Mutt's fur around the animal's face before pushing Mutt away and standing up. He held out his hand and pulled Edward to his feet, aiding his lover in dusting down the back of his pants and shirt.

"You ready to go in?" Jamie asked Edward.

"I suppose if we must," Edward said. "Shouldn't stand our hosts up."

Jamie kissed Edward again. "Plus, I'm fucking hungry." He grinned. In his hunt for Edward, he'd left the hotel via the kitchen and damn had it all smelled so good.

Edward laughed and brushed at his pants. "Well that won't do," he said. He ran his hands up and over Jamie's chest, resting them on Jamie's shoulders. "Thank you for looking for me."

"Thank you for not killing me," Jamie teased.

Nodding, Edward leaned in for another kiss and then, taking Jamie's hand, guided him toward the entrance.

"Wait," Jamie said. He looked back to where Mutt was sitting beside the gazebo. The dog was tied to the railing and had the most pathetic look on his face. "We can't leave him out here."

"Why?" Edward asked. "He has shade and water."

"But look at him." Mutt looked at them with his big brown eyes, and Jamie's heart melted. The dog was so damn cute.

Edward sighed. "Fine. But you should check with Lucas before you bring him into the dining room. He won't want you feeding the thing off your plate and starting bad habits." Edward paused and folded his arms across his chest. "The last thing anybody needs is that animal disrupting a wedding breakfast looking for people to feed it. And by anybody, I mean me."

"Okay. Okay." Jamie went back and untied Mutt. He

held the dog by the makeshift leash. "Who's a gorgeous boy?" he said and reached down to ruffle the fur on Mutt's head.

"No," Edward instantly said.

"What?" Jamie asked. He quirked an eyebrow and came to stand next to Edward.

"You don't want one."

Laughing, Jamie shook his head. "I never said I did."

"Uh-huh." Edward looked down at the dog. "Well, good. Because we're not getting one." There was a glimmer of warmth in Edward's eyes as he stared at the animal. Was it possible the uptight wedding planner was going soft?

Jamie moved forward and rested his chin on Edward's shoulder. He curled down his bottom lip and looked up at Edward.

"Cute, but I said no," Edward said. He glanced at Jamie and his lips twitched, a smile tweaking the corner of his mouth. "Oh stop it." He laughed and playfully pushed Jamie away. He met Jamie's eyes and sighed. "You're doing it on purpose, aren't you?"

Leaning in, Jamie kissed him. How he loved to tease Edward. "I don't want a dog," he said.

"You don't?" Edward narrowed his eyes.

Jamie shook his head. As nice an idea as it was, getting a dog just wasn't practical at the moment. "We both work and we can be out of the house all day. It wouldn't be fair." He rested his hands on Edward's waist. "But, maybe when we're old and crinkly and sitting at home in our armchairs with blankets on our knees, maybe then."

Edward's eyes brightened and then he lowered his head. With a small smile, he looked up at Jamie through his lashes. "You want to be with me when I'm old and crinkly?" Edward eventually said.

Nodding, Jamie reached up and gently nudged Edward's glasses up his nose. "Yep. Old and crinkly and bald," he said with a smirk.

Seemingly instinctively, Edward reached up and brushed his dark hair behind his ear. "Then I guess we should make the most of these." He ran his hands down Jamie's chest and lingered over his firm stomach. Jamie tensed his muscles and Edward sighed happily. It wasn't like Edward was out of shape. He was slim and tanned and suitably toned for his body type. But he was rather taken with Jamie's sculpted physique and had told Jamie so on more than one occasion.

"We really should," Jamie said. "But, later." He kissed Edward again and patted his stomach. "Food is calling."

Edward laughed. "Food. Is that all you think about?"

Jamie turned and walked backward a few steps. "Nope." He grinned as his gaze drifted to Edward's crotch.

"You're such a tosser," Edward said softly.

Holding out his hand, Jamie waited for Edward to catch up. The feel of Edward's fingers beneath his was one of the best feelings. Okay, so sex and kisses and heated touches were all damn amazing, but there was nothing quite as romantic as loosely holding Edward by the hand and swinging his arm as they walked.

"An adorable tosser," Edward added. He took Jamie's hand and they headed back to the hotel.

## Chapter Nine

EDWARD CURLED UP AGAINST JAMIE ON THE COUCH IN the lounge and eyed the completed tree. It wasn't so bad, he guessed, and it certainly gave off the homely feel he was sure the others had been going for. He had gotten so used to planning everything to perfection, he thought he'd maybe forgotten how to do things badly and just for fun. The tree was awash with fairy lights and decorations of different colors. He eyed one of the baubles on the bottom of the tree. Maybe if he just hung it on the branch above then it would placate the itch in his fingers to strip the tree bare and start over. No. He shouldn't. There was no order or scheme to the display, and as he watched the three strings of lights flash each to their own beat, he decided maybe just this once he could say *what the hell*. Jamie had often told him that learning to let go sometimes wasn't going to kill him.

*But the bauble…* Edward closed his eyes.

"You okay?" Jamie said. He gently rubbed Edward's arm.

Opening his eyes, Edward looked up at Jamie and nodded. "Just a little tired. Someone kept me awake last night." He grinned and hugged Jamie's arm.

"More like all those potato skins you ate." Jamie teasingly prodded at Edward's stomach.

The food Adam had put on had been lovely, and Edward had taken a liking to the warm cheese and chive potato skins as well as the vegetable samosas. Too many carbs and overindulgence left Edward feeling sleepy and full. But that was the point of Christmas, right? Eat too much, drink too much, and have plenty of fun and cheer. *And sleep, I hope.* Glancing at his watch, Edward was surprised to find it was after four. Had they really been eating for the last two hours? Urgh, he didn't want to see another mouthful until tomorrow. He looked to where Dylan was sitting on the other side of the room with Lucas and the dog. Edward snorted a laugh as he caught Dylan sneaking the animal something off his plate. So much for Lucas's rules.

"So, when do you head to your folks?" Dylan asked Jamie.

Jamie shifted a little as he straightened up, and Edward reluctantly sat up as well. "We'll stay here for Christmas Day and then head out before lunch the day after. Will that be okay?" He clearly felt he should check. After all, it would be either Dylan or Scott who would have to take them over to Marsh Harbor on *Liberty*.

"Yeah, yeah. Scott will be up early, I imagine." A grin spread over Dylan's face as he looked across the room. Scott hadn't been listening and looked up from the slab of chocolate cake he was eating.

Edward raised an eyebrow. How was Scott still eating? Where the hell did the man put it all?

"What?" Scott said. He looked from Dylan to Jamie and then to Adam. "What's going on?"

"Jamie and Edward have a flight at six am after Christmas so you'll be okay taking them, yeah?" Adam informed him with a smirk.

Scott nodded his head. "Yeah, sure," he quickly agreed though it was clear as he looked at Adam his brain was just catching up. "Wait. Wha'?"

"Don't worry, baby," Adam said. He cupped Scott's face and pulled him into a kiss. "We're just playing." He wiped away the chocolate smudge at the corner of Scott's mouth. With a shrug, Scott returned to his cake.

"Anyone want any more?" Adam asked. He pushed himself off the floor and onto his knees. He waited and looked around everybody. He received a few *no*s and shakes of heads. Tapping Scott's leg, he nodded to the leftover food. "Help me clear it up?"

Lucas raised his hand and indicated for Adam to

stay sitting down. "Don't worry about it. We'll do it. You've done plenty."

Adam said, "It's fine. We don't mind."

Through a mouth full of cake, Scott added, "Yeah, we don't mind."

"I'll give you a hand," Tasha piped up. She got to her feet and was instantly grabbing for Liam's hand. "Whoa." She cleared her throat. "Head rush." She laughed and glanced down at Liam, who wore a serious expression.

Edward decided enough was enough. Far too much syrupy politeness in one room. "How about we all do it?" Edward announced. He got to his feet and rested his hand on his hip. "Everyone grab some plates." He raised an eyebrow as he noted Mutt with a paper plate in his mouth. "Dylan, you can get that one." He pointed to the dog and the slobber-soaked more-like-a-lump-of-papier-mâché plate in its mouth.

"Gee, thanks," Dylan said and got up off the floor. He pulled at the plate, only for Mutt to have a seemingly vise-like grip on it. Suddenly, the dog was on its feet, its tail wagging as Dylan was now engaged in a game of tug of war. Edward did his best not to laugh as Dylan walked in circles. Pieces of the plate tore off as he struggled to get a grip on the whole thing.

"What are you doing?" Lucas asked and leaned forward. He grabbed Mutt by his collar and patted the dog's behind. Obediently, the dog sat down. "Give."

Lucas held out his hand and Mutt looked at him with those big brown eyes. Lucas seemed undeterred and repeated, "Give."

"He doesn't know what that means," Dylan insisted.

Lucas shot him a look. "Sure he does." He looked back at the dog. "Mutt, give." And sure enough, the dog lowered its head and opened its mouth, a clump of soggy plate falling into Lucas's hand.

Edward pressed a hand to his mouth. Just the thought of the slimy texture made him want to heave. "That's disgusting."

From the look on Lucas's face, it was as horrible as it looked. "Thanks," he said. He rubbed the dog's head and headed for the door.

"Okay then," Edward said. He'd get the group organized. "Everyone grab something and then we can regroup in thirty for drinks and games." He looked at Dylan. "There are games, right?"

Dylan chewed on his lip thoughtfully. "I think Tasha brought some." He looked at Tasha who nodded.

"I have Taboo, Pictionary, and Twister." Tasha picked up one of the empty serving trays and handed it to Liam. "Or I'm sure we can make up some of our own."

"Excellent." Edward turned around and pulled on Jamie's arm. "Come on."

Jamie sighed. "Games? Seriously?"

Pulling harder, Edward managed to move Jamie to

the edge of the couch. "Yes, seriously. And you better believe I intend to win." He looked at his boyfriend firmly.

"Fine," Jamie said in a low voice. "But if people start taking their clothes off, I'm out of here." He tensed his jaw and appeared uncomfortable. Though Edward didn't see the party heading in that particular direction, even with alcohol, he understood Jamie's hesitance to undress. The scars Jamie bore were reminders of horrible times. He'd fought for his country and its people and wasn't yet at a point where he wore them proudly as a badge of honor. Instead, they were just ugly memories. Luckily, in the bedroom it was a different story, just him and Edward and their private space. In some ways, both of them had their demons to overcome. Jamie's were just a hell of a lot more serious than the fear of getting dirty hands or messed-up hair.

Leaning over, Edward whispered, "You're beautiful."

Jamie looked up at him and there was so much love in his green eyes as he smiled.

Everyone else had already headed for the kitchen, and Edward took the opportunity to lose himself in a long kiss with Jamie. "Love you."

"ANYONE NEED A REFILL?" EDWARD ASKED. HE POURED himself a glass of wine and then held out the bottle.

"Tasha, would you like something a little stronger?"

Tasha shook her head. "I'm still full from lunch. I'll stick with the orange juice, thanks."

"Liam?"

Liam looked at his empty glass and screwed up his mouth. "I might have a beer."

"Oh, I'll have one of those. Cheers, Ed," Scott called from across the room.

*Ed? Dick.* "I wasn't—"

"Make that three," Lucas interrupted.

There was no point in arguing. "Anyone else?"

He met Jamie's eyes. "I'll have the wine," Jamie said. He held out his hand and waved Edward toward him to take the bottle.

"Lemonade for me," Adam said softly. His eyes held an apology as he joined in with the rest.

Dylan was suddenly at Edward's side, pressing the shorter rope he'd tied to the dog's collar in his hand. "Take Mutt with you and see he gets a drink."

If there was ever a time Edward regretted asking, now was it. He was relieved when Lucas took the leash and said, "I'll give you a hand."

"So," Edward asked as he and Lucas entered the kitchen. "You really okay about the dog?" He knew Lucas was of the same mind as him when it came to professionalism and perfection, well, in terms of pulling off the weddings on the Cay at least.

Lucas guided Mutt toward the back of the kitchen

and the bowl that was sitting by the door. "I think so," he said. He rubbed Mutt's back as the dog lapped at the water. "I mean, I wasn't sure at first, but it's not as bad as I thought." He looked fondly at the dog.

"It's only been a day," Edward pointed out. He met Lucas's eyes and suddenly felt bad. The dog was okay, he guessed. And man or animal, everybody deserved to be loved and looked after. "But you're right." He got the beers from the fridge and set them on the kitchen counter. "It's not bad. Actually, it's nice and sweet and…" Edward sighed. "He's like part of the family." He smiled at Lucas. "The three of you look good together."

Lucas laughed and rubbed his hand around Mutt's ears. "Don't go telling Dylan that. I just have this horrible feeling he's getting attached and then someone's going to have reported him missing and want him back."

"Oh yeah. Dylan mentioned you'd reported it to the police." Edward didn't see the point. The dog had clearly been mistreated and living on the street for God knows how long.

With a sigh, Lucas straightened up. "You never know. There might be somebody looking for him."

Surprising himself, Edward felt a twinge of sadness at the thought of having to hand the dog over. "I guess." He found a clean glass and poured the lemonade. "You will keep an eye on him when the Crofts and their guests are here, yeah?"

"Of course," Lucas said. In a world where anyone with a computer and access to the internet could write a review, Edward knew the last thing Lucas would ever want to do was give someone a reason to write a bad one. "Dylan's going to look into kennels and fencing and giving him a space in our living area. You won't even know he's here."

Edward smiled. "Okay." He opened the fridge and took out the fresh orange juice. "Talking weddings, any news on yours?"

Lucas leaned against the breakfast bar and shrugged. "Honestly, it's not something we've talked about recently." He lowered his head and rubbed at his eye. "I guess that's a good thing." Slowly, he twisted the silver band he wore on his finger and smiled. "Means we're happy just the way we are. And we are," Lucas insisted.

"Good," Edward said firmly. If he was honest, he wasn't sure if he'd ever get married. He knew of couples where the wedding was actually the beginning of the end. All the money people spent and all the stress of the lead-up and the day itself just didn't live up to the fantasy for some people. Sure he envied Dylan and Lucas a little with the whole wedding plan thing, but he didn't feel like he needed marriage with Jamie. Although that could change. He had Jamie, his forever guy. But he was also very much a 'don't fix it if it isn't broken' kind of guy.

"I promise, you'll be the first to know," Lucas said. He glanced down as Mutt came to his side. "That everything?" He nodded toward the drinks.

Edward mentally checked the list in his head. "Yeah. I got Dylan a beer. That okay?"

"Yup." Lucas brought Mutt with him and then looked between the leash and the drinks.

Laughing, Edward picked up the two glasses and one of the beers. "I'll come back." If Mutt continued to be as excitable as he had been, chances were Lucas would be wearing the drinks.

Two trips and a few minutes later, Edward settled back on the couch. Sipping his wine, he waited as Tasha decided what they were going to play next. Pictionary had been interesting, particularly Scott's drawing of a pepper mill that looked more like a cock, and in a game of Who Am I? Lucas thought he was so funny sticking a post-it on Edward's forehead and making him the Queen of England. He just hoped it wasn't Twister next. He wasn't feeling all that bendy after so much food and drink.

"So, we're going to play our own version of the Newlyweds game," Tasha enthused. "We'll be in our couples and it's to see which couple knows each other the best. I've got some questions and you can write your answers down and see if they match up."

Edward looked at Jamie. How was this game fair? Scott and Adam had known each other for forever, Dylan and Lucas were practically married, and Liam and Tasha *were* married. Edward felt underprepared. What kind of questions? Like, what was Jamie's favorite color? Was he supposed to know that? Had Jamie ever told him?

"Who wants to go first?"

"Here," Jamie said.

Edward tried his best not to look horrified when Jamie raised his hand. Clearly, the man was drunk.

Jamie took the paper and pens from Tasha and sat back down. He smiled as he met Edward's eyes and leaned in to kiss him. "Don't worry. It doesn't matter if you don't know all the answers." He handed Edward one of the pens and pads of paper. "We just have to get enough to beat Scott and Adam." Grinning, he shuffled over a cushion to put some space between them on the couch.

"No cheating," Scott chimed.

Edward shot him a look. Cheating? Oh it was so on. "We'll be fine," he said firmly and turned to Tasha. "First question please."

"Okay. You'll both need to write down an answer. So, starting with something simple, what is Jamie's favorite color?"

Bollocks.

# Chapter Ten

DYLAN SAT BACK ON THE SOFA AND WAITED FOR LUCAS to come back. They'd agreed to sit together and look at the letters, and by tacit agreement they decided it would just be them at first. Somehow Lucas felt the same as him—that whatever was in there was special.

He hadn't brought the laptop with him for the notes, but that wasn't the purpose of tonight. Now was all about learning more about PF, Peter French, and his possible lover Alfie J.

"Okay?" Lucas placed two hot chocolates on coasters, then pressed a switch so that instead of random patterns in the tree lights they sat on one color. The glow of purple leant a surreal glow to the entire room.

Dylan smiled up at his lover. "Nervous a bit, I think, and intrigued."

Lucas sat next to him and turned sideways so he could see Dylan.

"So the first letter is 1935?"

"And the last one is eight years later."

"How many in all?"

Dylan didn't have to count them again, he'd already thumbed his way through the pile of faded envelopes. "Seventeen."

"So how are we doing this? You want to take one each or we just read one at a time?"

"One at a time," Dylan decided. Reverently, he pulled apart the ribbon and gently lifted the first letter.

"More light," Lucas said softly as he flicked on the lamp next to the sofa.

Dylan nodded his agreement, then eased out the sheet of paper inside before unfolding it with only the tips of his fingers. The paper was stronger than he'd thought it would be. At least it didn't fall apart in his hands. Peering closely, he made out the writing that was bold in its style but faint from the years.

"*My darling, Alfie,*" Dylan began. "*I cannot begin to tell you what it meant to me that you decided to remain at the Cay for a whole week even after the incident with Annalisa. I may have no choice in my future, but I will always have the Cay. It pains me to admit the beach is a distant memory, but the touch of you and the love I have for you is something I will forever remember.*"

Dylan paused as he peered closer at the next

sentence. The words were pale and difficult to read. It seemed that the writing on the reverse had merged with some of the writing on the front. Dylan supposed an expert may well be able to decipher what each side said but to the naked eye it was impossible.

"So this really is a love letter then to Alfie. Who is it signed by, does that give us a clue?"

"*Yours, Peter,*" Dylan said softly. "Two men."

"No initial with the Peter?" Lucas lifted the envelope and tilted it to the light. There was no return address, only a small shell shape doodled in the bottom left hand corner. "No F for French," he said sounding disappointed.

"The letter does mention Annalisa who I assume is the Bainbridge that Peter marries in that Wikipedia article. Which makes me think that this is the same Peter French who died twenty years ago. I researched the names, but nothing has surfaced anywhere saying that the millionaire Peter French was gay. He and Annalisa divorced on grounds of infidelity from what I could see. His, not hers, in 1942."

Dylan slipped letter one back in its envelope, hoping to hell letter two was saved more from the ink bleed than the first one.

"You want to keep going?" Lucas asked carefully.

"Yeah. Just a couple more." He laid the first letter to one side on the sofa and picked up the second. The same shell was in the corner, and when he glanced through the rest it was on every one of the envelopes. "You think it's some secret love sign or something."

"Possibly. Could be linked to the shell we found in the case."

"Okay, here goes with this one. *My darling, Alfie. It has been too long and I crave your touch and I am going mad without you. The madness is a sickness I wish I could cure with your kisses. I often think of you when I am alone and it is the only peace I have in a world where I am expected to be the other half of a couple where my wife knows I live a lie. Annalisa suspects I write these letters for reasons other than I tell her. I neither confirm nor deny, but I see she is desperately sad. I wish to God I had it in me to feel sorrow for what I am doing in staying out of her bedroom, but she is not, nor will she ever be, you.*"

"Is there more?"

"I am struggling to read this. I think there was water inside the box. Something about a party and a liaison, I think it says liaison." Dylan turned the page over and in the margin, saved from the ravages of seawater and time, there was a small picture. Two stick figures in an obviously sexual pose, one on all fours, the other behind. There was some tiny dots next to it which probably once was writing. "There's something here about…wait…*photo from that day…*blurred there… *enclosed for you to recall every moment of our happiness reflected in your eyes.*"

Lucas picked up the picture of the smiling man with the name Alfie and 1935. "This photo, I guess," he said.

They continued reading. A couple of the letters were completely ruined, but the closer they got to the last one, the more passionate the writing. Words and sentences jumped off the page. *I will always love you. I hate this lie of a marriage.*

"Poor guys never had a chance to be together for real," Dylan said.

"You think anyone else would want to read these?"

"Depends if either of them had family. Evidently Peter French had no one in his life. His brother was the one who had a wife and kids, the ones who carried on the Foundation's work under Peter's name. We don't know about Alfie. Look at this, *"She is expecting our child, I am horrified that I have let it go this far, am I wrong to want nothing of this baby?"*

"That's so sad. Do you think Annalisa knew that Peter was in love with someone else?"

Dylan shook his head. "I don't know. We can't tell from these."

Lucas unfolded another and scanned the contents. "She lost the baby," he said quietly. "A miscarriage, so Peter tells Alfie." He handed the letter over to Dylan, who read the contents carefully. Some words were smudged but the intention in the writing was clear.

*This is my fault, I killed that baby by wishing the child had never been conceived.* The writing was harsh and lacked the romantic tones that Peter had written before.

"Oh God, that's so sad."

"The rest is too faint." Dylan picked up the final letter and opened it as carefully as he could. Dated December 1943, it appeared to answer a letter Alfie had written telling Peter he had been called to war.

"Called or volunteered?" Lucas speculated out loud.

"Doesn't say, just that Peter is devastated and calls on Alfie to be careful, to stay alive. That he's sorry as well, about what he said in connection with the baby. Look." Dylan carefully followed the writing with his finger just above the thin paper. "*Our marriage is done. Annalisa has fallen for another and they appear happy. Her father hates that our marriage ceased, but to her credit, she refuses to tell anyone what I told her about us. She says we deserve our happiness, that she always knew. I believe I have wronged her in thinking she was the same as others who would hate us. I've assumed all responsibility for the divorce, and she will be happy now I think. She imagines I will live on my island with you and I want that more than anything. The waterfall, our home, we could build a house solid into the rock and be happy forever.*

*To war? I wish I could fight alongside you, but I have again been refused entry. Even with all my money my eyesight fails me. But, as to us, the world is changing, Alfie, my darling. When this war is over, when you come home, it will be to a new world where our love will be free and unchallenged. Stay safe my love. Yours forever, Peter.*"

"Jesus, these are hard to listen to," Lucas said.

Dylan sighed. "This is one set of really unhappy letters. I can see where this is going. The letters stop in 1943. Alfie goes off to war and dies. Peter lives to be an old lonely man. There is no happy ending."

Lucas leaned into him. "We don't know Alfie died."

"Well, no one came back for the box," Dylan explained his reasoning and punctuated it with a shrug.

"These two men found each other in a time when it wasn't easy to be together, they were happy with catching whatever time they could in the years they were in love. Anyway, it isn't always about the happy ending," Lucas offered. "Sometimes it's about the journey."

"Are you trying to make a point? We're happy, aren't we? Don't you think we have our happy ending?" Dylan felt concerned at the oddly resigned tone Lucas was using.

"Don't be stupid, of course I do. These two though, they had time on the Cay, that is what I meant. I wasn't talking about us."

"Well maybe we should." Dylan didn't mean to sound irritable or even sad, but he could hear both in his voice. Quickly, before Lucas could say a thing, Dylan leaned forward and kissed Lucas squarely on the lips.

Seemed Dylan's distraction techniques weren't working though when Lucas pulled back and eyed him suspiciously. "What's wrong?"

"Nothing," Dylan lied. He wanted to be able to put in words how he felt about Lucas, but sometimes the words just escaped him. "I think that in their time they couldn't be honest about who they loved. Agreed?"

"Alfie and Peter? No. Honesty about being homosexual wasn't something that happened in 1930s America."

"Not being honest about being gay," Dylan attempted to explain. "Honest about being in love, without the labels. We can, you know, we can marry, here on the island." He held up his ring finger. "But we don't. They never got the chance to be together, but we take it for granted that we can get married. We're wasting the possibilities and chances we have."

For a few seconds Lucas simply stared at Dylan. "Well, I didn't want to rush things."

"Neither did I," Dylan said.

"What I meant was I didn't want to rush you into something you'd regret, is all."

Dylan realized he probably looked like a guppy with his mouth opening and closing as he tried to form words. "I didn't want to push you, in case you wanted to change your mind."

Abruptly, it was Lucas's turn to be speechless. His

eyes widened in comic shock that probably mirrored what was on Dylan's face.

"This is stupid," Lucas finally said. "I love you."

"I love you too."

Lucas continued, "I never want us to end."

"I don't either."

"We're idiots."

Dylan nodded his head. "Agreed."

"Let's set a date, for real," Lucas decided. "But we wouldn't get away with a quiet wedding. You know Edward has these big plans."

For a second, Dylan was doubtful. He had pictured a quiet beach wedding with friends and Lucas's family. Pretty much like how it was now for Christmas Day. "I don't care what he does as long as it's with you and me ending the day as husbands." Some small thing niggled at the back of his head. His dad. He'd never come over for a wedding between his gay son and another man, but maybe Dylan should at least invite him and his girlfriend. Lucas pulled him from his musings with a question.

"So tomorrow we set a date with Edward?"

"Yeah. Definitely." Dylan was never more positive about anything as he was now.

"Get married as soon as we can."

Dylan nodded. "Soon sounds good."

.  .  .

THEY RE-READ A COUPLE OF THE OLDER LETTERS, BUT they were unbearably poignant when Peter talked about forever even though there were no letters after 1943.

"Maybe we should get this looked at by someone who can get both sides of the letters."

"Should we do that? I don't imagine the Bainbridge family or the French Foundation will be very happy to have written proof of something like this."

"Then maybe we could track down what happened to Alfie, look at his heirs if he had any, or sideways, nieces, nephews. Someone will want to have these memories. After New Years."

Dylan was distracted by his cell dancing across the highly polished table, and he picked it up without thinking. The name on the screen was a blast from the past. Mitch. His dad's assistant and the man who thought getting together with Dylan was a convenience they should try for. He argued with himself over whether he should answer it, but what if something had happened to his dad? Fear gripped him. He was sitting here contemplating getting back in touch with his dad, and meanwhile he could be dying. Pressing the connect button, he spoke first.

"Mitch. What's wrong? Is it Dad?"

"Dylan, that you?" Mitch's voice didn't sound right. Kind of slurred. "I need to book your island," he added.

Why was Mitch calling them on Christmas Eve? "What the hell, Mitch?"

"Got a new contract with models, lots of 'em, and I need an island. Then I thought, Dylan has a freaking island. And it's Christmas Eve and I was thinking about you. Not thinking about you really, just you were in my head. Right? Am I right? Or am I wrong?"

About being in Mitch's head or about the fact Dylan had an island? "It's nearly midnight on Christmas Eve, Mitch, why are you phoning me?"

Lucas leaned in to listen to the conversation. "Mitch? What's he want?" he mouthed.

Dylan shrugged, then placed a hand over the cell. "Think he's drunk-dialing me. Wants to hire the Cay."

"Dylan! My man, you still there?"

"Mitch, Merry Christmas and all, but you gotta phone me after January first, man."

"Oh. My bad. So can I have your island?"

"Lucas can check dates after New Years for you."

"Lucas. How is he? Still the love of your life?" Mitch didn't sound bitter, and why would he? Mitch and Dylan didn't really go anywhere.

"Goodbye, Mitch," Dylan said softly.

"Oh, okay then. Merry Christmas."

Suddenly, Mitch didn't sound so drunk. If anything, he sounded tired, and hell, was Mitch being a sad drunk on Christmas Eve? Why wasn't he with other people being all kinds of single and happy?

"Hang on. Mitch, what are you doing for Christmas?"

"Nothing special," Mitch said firmly. Either the alcohol was wearing off or he'd been exaggerating the effects to sound less stupid phoning Dylan this late at night on Christmas Eve.

"You seeing Dad?"

"I don't work for him anymore. Couldn't. Not after he got all soft on a client and refused to seal the deal. We argued, I walked. Didn't he tell you?"

*What deal? His dad was soft? That didn't sound right, Dylan's dad was hard-nosed and focused at all times.* "We don't talk much," Dylan admitted. Then he changed the subject. "What about spending Christmas with your brother?"

"He's in England with his new wife. I don't want to see anyone at Christmas. Jeez, Dylan, you getting slow in your old age playing house with that man of yours? We're not all settled down. Some of us like to play the field and enjoy ourselves."

"Uh-huh." Dylan refused to take offense. He was happy and he'd become *more* than just *alone* because he was with Lucas. He had love and a future, and now, his man was marrying him. He didn't expect Mitch to understand that. "Phone me in the New Year. And have a good Christmas, Mitch."

"You too."

Dylan ended the call and immediately leaned in to kiss a bemused Lucas. "Mitch. He'll phone us back in the New Year if you're okay with that."

"Why wouldn't I be okay? He's an ex with emphasis on the ex. I'm old enough to handle your past life." Lucas smirked as he said that. "Was he drunk?"

"Sounded like he was acting drunk to me, like that made it a reason to be calling me on Christmas Eve."

"You're feeling sorry for the guy," Lucas summarized.

"Well, who wouldn't? He's not exactly happy at any time. He's like a miniature version of my dad, all projects and deadlines and profit."

Dylan placed all the letters carefully on the table before straddling his husband on the sofa. They kissed deeply and Dylan leaned over to switch off the lamp until they were kissing in just the purple glow.

"I'm guessing you want to stop talking about Mitch and your dad," Lucas deadpanned.

Dylan deepened the kiss as his answer. He wanted nothing more than Lucas here and now. In fact this was his idea of perfect.

Utterly perfect.

## Chapter Eleven

LUCAS THOUGHT HE HAD NEVER SEEN SO MUCH wrapping paper in his life. Bright red Santas fought for dominance with enough scarlet ribbon to wrap around the entire Cay with some left over. Dylan didn't do things by halves, and it seemed that every Christmas the presents and the wrapping became more inventive.

"And it does what?" Lucas asked as he held up a handle that had five flexible prongs poking from the end. He was suspicious of what Dylan had called it and was convinced it was actually some kind of sex toy.

Dylan huffed and took the object from his hand then proceeded to demonstrate on his head. "You see?" he said with a grin. "It's soft and it massages your head."

"So it's not a sex toy," Lucas had to clarify.

"I promise you it's not," Dylan said with a firm tone. Then he leaned over the side of the bed, and for a long minute his ass was waving temptingly in Lucas's face clad only in the novelty boxers that Lucas had bought him. Proclaiming 'This way to heaven' right across his butt was enough to have Lucas collecting up the nearest paper in the vain hope the shorts would be coming off. His hope was short lived when Dylan pushed himself upright and handed over another gift. To Lucas's counting this was the tenth present this year, although this one wasn't wrapped in scarlet but a more sedate pale green. Lucas did what Dylan expected, he shook the parcel, sniffed it, then poked at it with a finger.

Their first Christmas together had been Lucas's introduction with the patented Dylan way of opening gifts. Lucas was horrified that Dylan unwrapped without the necessary appreciation of what could be inside. Lucas wanted Christmas to be perfect for Dylan, who was nothing more than a kid on Christmas Day and quickly got into the swing of things. He'd always tried to make Christmas good for Tasha after their parents died, but he hated the thought that he'd never managed to give her the one thing she'd always needed—a sense of fun.

"What's wrong?" Dylan asked, concerned.

Lucas blinked at his fiancé. Wrong? He realized he was simply staring down at the parcel and hadn't moved. "Nothing, sorry, I fazed out there, thinking about Tasha."

Dylan nodded. "You're worried about her too?" he said softly.

"No, I was thinking about…wait…you're worried about Tasha?"

"I'm sure it's nothing," Dylan offered, "I just think she looks quite pale and like she has lost a little weight is all."

"I noticed that. I put it down to office working and not seeing the sun. Do you think I should talk to her?" Silly question, of course he was going to talk to her. Sometimes he couldn't see for looking even when something was right in front of his face. Dylan had empathy and awareness and all those things Lucas had to work at to achieve.

"Later," Dylan reassured. "For now, we have ninety minutes until brunch and I really want you to open that gift so we can play." Dylan waggled his eyebrows and grinned and Lucas pushed to one side the instinct to go find his sister now. She was probably sleeping and enjoying her own lazy Christmas morning with Liam. He'd pull her aside after brunch and check in on her.

Finally, he levered the lid off the pale green box and stared down in amazement. The fattest, shortest…hell… he'd never seen a dildo quite like it. He knew his mouth was open. Was Dylan hoping this thing was going in Lucas's ass? Lucas poked at it. It wasn't stiff and unmoving, more like bendable but firm. Weird.

"Apparently, it's really good," Dylan enthused.

"Uh-huh," Lucas said, careful to skirt the whole fuck-that's-wide issue.

"You don't like it?" Dylan asked.

"I do, I just—"

"Great. Because…" Dylan went onto all fours and moved on the bed toward Lucas before lowering his voice. "If you use that in me you can keep me on the edge forever, and you know how much you love doing that."

Lucas looked at the dildo with a new appreciation. He loved stretching Dylan, keeping him so close to coming, sucking on his cock until Dylan was begging incoherently.

"That is one hell of a gift."

"It's more for me," Dylan said with a grin.

Dylan carefully moved all of their gifts off the bed and onto the floor, then pulled the short, wide dildo from the box. He grabbed lube, and then lying on his back, he tapped the dildo on his stomach.

"Whatcha waiting for, then?" he asked with a smirk.

Lucas was so hard just imagining using this on Dylan, and when they kissed he thought he could never be happier with this mix of lust and love that coursed through him. Moving down Dylan's body until he could take the weight of his fiancé's cock in his mouth, he hummed happily at the taste. He wasn't sure how he was supposed to be using this dildo. It surely wasn't long enough to tap at Dylan's prostate. Using enough lube to make everything slippery, he began to stretch Dylan first with fingers, then with the dildo, all while keeping his lips on Dylan's cock and worshipping it with licks and sucks. Whatever was happening to Dylan, Lucas decided he wanted some of it. Incoherently babbling and pleading, Dylan was curling up and demanding more.

Dylan was so stretched and wide, and when Lucas pulled the dildo out he could easily press four fingers inside. He crooked his finger and gently stroked Dylan's prostate and it was game over for Dylan in seconds. Lucas swallowed Dylan's release and nearly lost it himself when Dylan shouted. A few strokes of his hand and he was coming over Dylan's belly and chest. Just the thought of marking his lover made him insane.

"Forever," he muttered against Dylan's heated skin.

"Always," Dylan replied.

He and Dylan were last to arrive at brunch. Adam was the only one absent from the large breakfast table in the kitchen.

"Where's Adam?"

"He forgot cream for the coffee, he's in the fridge," Scott said helpfully.

"I said we should shut the door on him," Jamie smirked.

The table was full of plates containing crispy bacon,

scrambled eggs, pancakes, fruit, bread, butter, jams, and pastries.

Dylan groaned. "How are we expected to eat all of this, then dinner tonight?"

"You'll manage," Adam said from behind him. He placed cream at either end then took his place next to Scott. "Everyone start," he said. And boy did everyone start. There was good-natured fighting over bacon, and an egg fight broke out between Jamie and Adam. Lucas had to laugh when both Scott and Edward watched their partners with smiles on their faces. He kept looking back at Tasha who was chatting with Liam. She didn't appear so pale today, and there was a wash of color in her cheeks. She didn't have much food on her plate, some strawberries and a couple of pancakes, but that could just as well be her first plate. Didn't mean she wouldn't eat more.

When Lucas helped himself to plate two and Tasha was still playing with the first strawberry, Lucas instinctively knew something was wrong. She never ate to the same level as he did, but even for her, this was unusual.

"Are you okay, Tasha?" he asked gently. She looked up at him and thankfully no one else at the table noticed their whispered conversation. Suddenly, it was just the two of them with the weight of a question hanging between them.

Tasha stood and excused herself. "Can I borrow you

a minute?" she said. Liam stood as well and the three of them left the room. As soon as they were outside in the hallway, Lucas repeated the question. *Please, don't let her be ill.*

"I'm pregnant, Lucas," she said with a smile. She gripped Liam's hand. "You're going to be an uncle."

Lucas didn't know what he'd been expecting, but it wasn't this. He knew Tasha wanted a family, but she hadn't told him they were trying or anything…or… He mentally smacked himself upside the head.

"Tash," he said and pulled her into his arms. "That is wonderful news." He grasped Liam and encouraged him into the group hug. "My baby sister is gonna be a mom," he said. "Congratulations, guys." He stood back and his eyes immediately zeroed in on her hands lying protectively over her stomach. "How far are you?"

"Just finishing the puking stage," she said with a wry grin. "Twelve weeks now."

"That's why you look tired, then? You not sleeping?"

"I'm just sick of being sick," she punned.

"What a wonderful Christmas present. Liam, I'm so pleased for both of you."

"Is everything okay?" Dylan said from the door. He looked worried.

"Can everyone else know?" Lucas asked quickly.

"We were going to tell everyone today anyway, I just wanted you to be the first to know."

Lucas held his sister close again and inhaled the citrusy scent in her hair. "I love you so much, little sis," he whispered into her ear.

Tasha chuckled. "Back at ya, big brother."

Together all three of them went back into the room, Lucas collecting Dylan in a hug on the way.

"We have an announcement," Liam said proudly. Everyone looked up expectantly. "We're having a baby. Due early July."

Lucas watched as Dylan hugged her close, and then she turned to Adam, Scott, and Jamie. Finally, Edward got his turn and Lucas heard him promise Tasha the best baby shower ever. He guessed he was an uncle, but these other men standing in this kitchen would be just as much part of his niece or nephew's life.

Tasha smiled and laughed and Lucas couldn't be prouder of his little sister.

"You okay?" Dylan asked from his side. "You're looking a bit shocked."

"I'm so blown away that I am going to be an uncle. That we are going to be uncles," he corrected himself.

Dylan hugged him from the side. "We'll be cool uncles. The ones who have a whole island for a kid to play on. And a dog. We have a dog."

Lucas melted inside. Dylan sounded as full of awe as Lucas was. Family was important. Vital. Standing here in this kitchen was every little part of his family.

"I'm going to call Dad after this," Dylan said soft enough so that only Lucas could hear.

"Are you sure?" While Lucas wanted this more than anything, to see Dylan able to heal some old wounds, he selfishly wanted Dylan to himself today. And how stupid was that? After all, it had been he who had opened lines of communication with Dylan's father.

"I'm ready," Dylan admitted.

"You want me to be there when you do it?"

Dylan squeezed him hard and pressed a kiss into his hair. "Of course I want you there, but I won't ask you to be there. I need to do this on my own. Thank you for wanting to hold my hand, but I'm a big boy now."

Everyone had settled back at the table, and Edward was in full-on organizing mode. From cribs to color schemes, the planner was doing what he did best, planning. Jamie looked at him every so often with a mix of exasperation and love on his face. Lucas sat back at the table and couldn't help the grin on his face. He was months away from being an uncle. Just months.

Brunch out of the way and the kitchen tidied to within an inch of its life, Adam shooed them out of the space and told them he would be ready to serve dinner at seven that evening. Everyone had hours to fill and Lucas was torn between staying with Jamie and Scott, who were talking waterskiing, or Edward, who had his diary out and was feverishly writing notes, or just sitting with Tasha and Liam. The decision became simple when Tasha and Liam disappeared to their room.

He just wanted to know how Dylan was getting on, and at least listening to Scott argue why the Cay was the perfect place to water-ski and all they needed was a boat was a distraction. He glanced at his watch. Dylan had been gone twenty minutes now. How long did it take to wish someone Merry Christmas?

Long enough, he guessed, to make up for lost time. Hours probably.

He hoped to hell it was going okay.

## Chapter Twelve

*MAN UP ALREADY*. DYLAN HAD HIDDEN HIMSELF AWAY IN the office over twenty minutes ago, and he knew it wouldn't be long before Lucas or someone came searching for him. How hard was it to make a damn phone call? Very, it seemed. Okay, so he'd told Lucas he was going to call his dad to wish him a Merry Christmas, but when it came down to it, he still had the same hang-ups. Would he still hear the hint of disapproval in his father's voice about Dylan's life and about the choices he'd made? He wasn't sure he and his dad had ever really addressed the whole gay thing properly due to the lack of conversation between the two of them. Was that yet another disappointment for his father and going to cause more hurt for him?

Taking a deep breath, Dylan tapped in his father's

digits. He held the phone to his ear and listened to the tone as he waited for his call to connect. The few short rings felt like an eternity, and he was tempted to claim he'd tried and just hang up.

"Hello." The voice belonged to a woman, and Dylan was suddenly lost for words. His father'd had a string of girlfriends after his mom died. None of those relationships had staying power back then, but in recent years his father had mellowed and just maybe he'd found a companion who could stay the distance.

"Rebecca, Merry Christmas," Dylan said. He hoped he'd gotten it right. If it was the same woman he remembered his father dating, he'd actually met her once. If he recalled right, she and his father had been together for four years now.

"Yes?"

"It's Dylan. Is Dad there?"

"Oh, Dylan. Merry Christmas to you, too. And yeah, your Dad's right here." Her voice lowered as she held the phone away and called to Dylan's father. "D, it's for you." He could hear his father's voice in the background in answer. He couldn't believe someone was calling Dylan Hector Gray Senior by the nickname D, but it seemed like Rebecca was managing it. "He's on his way. He's getting old and can't get off the couch." She laughed and Dylan relaxed. He'd built making the call into some terrible thing, but really, it was just people and conversation. There was nothing there that could truly hurt him.

"So, how are you?" she asked. "And how's that man of yours? I bet it must be lovely out there on the island for Christmas. Nothing but rain here for the last couple of days."

Christ the woman could talk, but Dylan found it comforting. "Yeah, it's nice. You should come out." He stopped. Had he just said that?

"Sounds great," Rebecca enthused. "Your father mentioned an invite or something but what with the operation and—" She halted. "Oh, he's made it. Anyway, it was lovely hearing from you. You should come visit. We're always saying we needed to invite you over. You could meet my two and their kids. You'd love the twins. How's Lucas with kids? Anyway, I'm being shooed. We really should do that. I'll get your dad to work a date with you."

"Erm, yeah, sure." Dylan reached up and gently curled his hair around his finger. Had he missed the stage he and his father had started building bridges? Maybe Rebecca was just being nice. And kids? The notion of his father playing granddad was beyond bizarre.

"Bye," she said.

A beat, and then his father was on the phone. "Dylan." Even from a single word, his father sounded as formal as ever. "Is everything okay? Do you need money?"

Dylan tensed. "No, Dad. I just wanted to call and wish you a Merry Christmas." He hadn't needed his father's money in all these years, as if he would start asking now.

"Well, thank you," Dylan Senior said oh so very carefully, like he'd been handed a grenade and it was going to explode at any moment. Clearly, he was waiting for the *but* in this conversation. "I wasn't expecting to hear from you."

Familiar feelings resurfaced in Dylan as he listened to his father's voice—anger, hate, bitterness. But they were also tinged with something else, the need to be loved and the need for family. In the last three years, Dylan had made his own family. He had Lucas and therefore Tasha and Liam and soon a nephew or niece. He had Scott, Edward, and Dominiq, all as good as any brother. But he guessed, despite all the people and love in his life, there was nothing that could quite match the love of his own father, of blood, especially a love he had always strived to gain when he was growing up.

"How are you?" Dylan asked. He'd eventually worked up the courage to ask Lucas about his father's operation. Seemed after years of wait and see, doctors had advised an operation for a hernia.

"Fine, fine. You?"

"Good, thank you." Dylan pinched the bridge of his

nose as he leaned back in his office chair. "How's your day been?"

"Good. I got your card."

Card? *Lucas.* Dylan had never been one for cards and address books.

His dad continued, "Rebecca's youngest and his family are joining us for dinner." He paused. "I would have liked to have seen you this year."

Dylan's brain stalled. "Really?" He hoped he didn't sound as incredulous as he felt about his father's statement.

Clearing his throat, Dylan Senior said, "I'm not getting any younger, son. I want you to know that she would have been proud of you, your mother. And that I'm proud of you. That I..." He struggled to finish his sentence.

*Fuck.* Panic swept through him, churning with fear as it hit the pit of his stomach. Was his dad holding back? Was there something more seriously wrong with him than just a hernia?

"Dad, are you okay?"

"I'm fine, son. I've just had time to think since Lucas's letter." The formal edge slipped, and Dylan swore he heard warmth in his father's voice. "Rebecca's had the grandkids over a few times and it's made me stop and take a look at my life."

An ache spread through Dylan's chest. All Dylan had ever wanted growing up was for his father to spend time with him, to tell him he loved him and offer him some glimmer of hope that he didn't blame Dylan for his wife's death.

"I wanted to tell you how sorry I am. Losing your mother, I just—"

"It's okay, Dad. You don't have to explain." Other family members had always commented how like his mother Dylan was, from his looks down to his free-spirited soul.

His father breathed into the phone, and Dylan could imagine him rubbing his creased brow. "Just tell me I'm not too late?"

Twenty-seven years was a long time to forgive. Dylan pressed his hand to his chest and rubbed the space above his heart. There had always been something missing, a small space that nothing could fill. Time to swallow his pride. "You're not," he said. It wasn't all on his father, he knew that. Dylan had never wanted to make it easy for the man, certainly not once he hit adulthood. "We're not."

***

LUCAS LEANED BACK IN THE LOUNGER ON THE POOLSIDE and stared up at the sky through his shades. Closing his eyes, he listened to the sound of playful laughter of Jamie, Scott, and Adam in the pool and tried to relax. Dylan had yet to emerge from the office, and despite

Lucas's best efforts to sit outside the door waiting to wrap his fiancé in a hug when he did, Scott and Jamie had convinced everyone to take the celebrations outside. So here he was, sunbathing and doing his best not to think about how Dylan was getting on or get irked by the fact Mutt had ended up in the pool with the rest of them. If dog hairs started clogging up the filter, he'd just have to talk to Dylan about hiring themselves a new pool boy.

"How would you feel about Joanne?" Tasha asked. She was sitting on the lounger beside him and had a glass of fruit juice cocktail Scott had mixed for her in her hand.

Lucas opened his eyes and turned his head to look at her. "Like Mom?"

"Mmm. If it's a girl. Or maybe as a middle name. So *something* Joanne, just haven't decided on the *something* yet." She pulled her leg up and rested her drink against it. In her swimsuit, Tasha's bump was more obvious, but if he hadn't known she was pregnant, he might have thought she was merely gaining a little weight around her stomach.

"And if it's a boy?" he asked. "Would you use Dad's name?"

Tasha smiled but shook her head. "Frank just doesn't seem quite right." She laughed. "We like Liam's grandfather's name, Oliver. Ollie. So we're thinking Oliver Lucas." She met his eyes briefly and then looked away and toward the pool where Liam had joined the others in some strange water-based game involving a soccer ball.

A smile curled the corner of Lucas's mouth. *Oliver Lucas*. He looked back at the sky. Heat spread across his face and he wasn't sure if it was the sun or the sense of pride that warmed him through. He let out a deep breath and made himself comfortable. He listened to the sounds of the men playing in the water and frowned as they suspiciously fell quiet. He could hear the movement of water, but the men's voices fell away. Lifting his head, he pushed his sunglasses up onto his head. Instinctively, he raised his hands as he spotted Mutt on the pool side and Jamie and Scott running awkwardly away through the water.

There was no time to move as Mutt shook the water from his coat. Tasha yelped beside him as cool water sprayed across them. The soccer ball then hit Lucas in the chest and Mutt bounded forward. Lucas was winded as the dog jumped up for the ball at his side and, as it rolled to the floor, decided he'd much rather be licking Lucas's face.

"Get off me." Lucas leaned away and pushed at the dog's chest. He managed to move Mutt and get the dog back to the floor. Wiping his face, he looked at the pool. Edward was sitting on the pool edge with his feet in the water and had a look of pure horror on his face. In the pool, the men were in hysterics.

"Yeah, so funny," Lucas said. He picked the ball up and slung it at Scott who caught it.

"Get in here, old man," Scott said and laughed.

*Old man?* "Nice," Lucas retorted. So he was a few years older than the rest of them. It didn't mean he was old. "I guess you won't be wanting your present after dinner when everyone else is opening theirs."

Scott beamed and was caught off guard by Adam as he jumped on his back. With a splash, the pair of them toppled back into the pool and went under the water. Edward flinched as water splashed up at him and tried to get to his feet as Jamie pounced in his direction and grabbed him by the ankles. Jamie's T-shirt rode up, and Lucas caught a short glimpse of the scars Jamie tried so hard to hide. One day he may truly relax in front of his friends. There was a strange sound as Edward was pulled into the water. Had Edward just screamed very much like a girl?

"What's going on?" Dylan said from behind Lucas.

It was as if a huge weight lifted from Lucas's chest as he caught sight of his lover. "Dylan?"

Dylan wore a bright smile as he looked at the chaos erupting in the pool. "Should I even ask?"

Laughing, Lucas shook his head. "Probably not." He held out his hand and sighed happily as Dylan took it and crouched beside the lounger. "You okay?" Lucas asked and squeezed Dylan's hand.

It took a moment but eventually, Dylan nodded. "I

think so." He looked at Lucas, seemingly examining every inch of his face.

"What?" Lucas asked.

"Nothing," Dylan said whimsically. He reached up and gently wiped at Lucas's nose. "Just some water."

Smiling, Lucas pulled Dylan into a brief hug. "What did you guys talk about?" he asked.

Dylan shrugged. "Just… We caught up. Talked about the island and you and how we've been doing. About him and work and his girlfriend and her family. She has grandkids." He met Lucas's eyes. "I feel exhausted from talking. But also…" He shook his head. "I don't know. But it's not a bad feeling." He laughed softly as he spoke. "I'm rambling, aren't I?"

"You can ramble all you want to," Lucas said. Sitting up, he held Dylan's hand in his lap. As long as Dylan was happy, that was all he cared about. He'd been so torn about what he had done. Yes, he'd gone behind Dylan's back, but he hated seeing Dylan shut out his own flesh and blood. From what Lucas could tell, he had been just like Dylan's father once upon a time—all work and no time to live.

"Thank you," Dylan said. "I know I didn't say it before, in fact, the opposite. But thank you."

"I'm glad it worked out okay, but I'm sorry I wasn't upfront about what I did. It won't happen again. I promise."

Dylan smiled and got to his feet. He pulled on

Lucas's hand, encouraging him to stand. Together, Dylan kissed him and wrapped his arms around Lucas's waist. "It's a good thing you're a good fuck," he said in a low voice. The gravelly growl went straight to the head of Lucas's dick, which pressed uncomfortably against the inside of his shorts. Hell, he'd be needing a cold shower if Dylan carried on like this. He looked up into Dylan's eyes as Dylan pressed his thigh into the space between his legs, catching his erection. Dylan's eyes brightened as he smiled, and Lucas realized they were moving. He realized too late where he was headed and toppled back when Dylan released him and shoved at his chest.

Emerging from the water, Lucas pulled off his sunglasses and pulled back his wet hair. He shielded his face as, still dressed in his T-shirt and cutoffs, Dylan jumped into the pool beside him. He waited for Dylan to reappear but was distracted as, en masse, the other men in the pool tackled him back under the water. Batting away their hands, he swam for the side and caught his breath. Shaking away the water, he looked up at Tasha, catching sight of her amused expression.

"Having fun?" she asked.

Lucas simply rolled his eyes and leaned back as Dylan wrapped his arms around his chest. Dylan pressed kisses to his neck and spun him around in the water to kiss him properly. He held onto Dylan and they met in an openmouthed kiss. He could hear the chants and cheers from the other men as they lost themselves in each other. Everything melted away except for him and Dylan.

Pulling back, they looked into each other's eyes. "I love you," Lucas mouthed, and Dylan pulled him close and kissed him again.

## Chapter Thirteen

LUCAS HELPED ADAM SET THE LAST DISH ON THE TABLE, then stood back with him to survey what they had laid out.

"Looks good," Scott said with a grin from the door. He'd been banished from the room since he was just following Adam around like a lost puppy.

"You don't think it's too much?" Adam worried his lower lip even as Scott came over and hugged him from behind. Candles flickered in the tiny alcoves around the room and in the burners below the gleaming serving dishes piled high with Christmas food.

"Way too much," Lucas pointed out as he stole a piece of buttery carrot. "Don't worry, it'll go," he muttered around the hot vegetable. "You can rely on Dylan and Scott."

"Did I hear my name?" Dylan joined them and slid

into a chair before shuffling close to the table. When he realized no one was saying anything, he looked up, bewildered.

Lucas shook his head. "You had to be first in."

Dylan shrugged. "I finished walking Mutt, gave him some of those pork rind things that Adam made, and figured I'd timed it right for eating. Anyway, I need to get to the turkey before Scott does, otherwise I'll never get a look in."

As each couple arrived, they spent time admiring the table, and Lucas couldn't help staring directly at Dylan and seeing the restlessness in his fiancé's expression. He really wanted to dig into the food that Adam had so carefully prepared. When they finally all dived into bowls of vegetables, platters of meat, sweet potatoes, rolls, gravy, and cranberry sauce, Lucas looked at the people that made up the table. Adam was beaming with a smile so wide he couldn't help but make Lucas smile in return. He was happy and excited, and from the way Scott kept staring at him, it would seem everything was good in the Scott/Adam camp. The more things that Adam did like this, the better his self-esteem would be.

Jamie was quiet, but then he had a plate filled almost as high as Dylan and was concentrating hard on trying to get through it. Every so often Edward would nudge his lover and they would exchange soft words Lucas couldn't hear. Edward's plate was a little more conservative, laid out with precision. Turkey and cranberry on the right, vegetables on the left, a sausage at the bottom, and gravy in a careful lake at the top. He even ate with careful consideration, but that was Edward all over. Tasha didn't have much on her plate, well not much other than turkey. Apparently, the baby wanted turkey, at which announcement the entire table broke down in laughter. Liam spoke easily to Edward and Jamie. It was like one big happy family.

He tapped his glass until everyone looked his way. "This time next year…" he started. He lifted his glass full of orange juice and champagne. "There will be a new baby in the family. To Tasha and Liam." He raised his glass and everyone copied.

"To Tasha and Liam."

Dylan pushed his chair back and lifted his glass high. "And this time next year…Lucas and I will be married."

Silence. Edward's eyes widened. "You set a date?" he asked immediately. Leaning down, he picked up his ever-present diary and flicked to May. "May fourth." he said firmly.

"May the fourth be with you," Scott sniggered. Adam thumped him, but Lucas agreed, May the fourth was kind of funny.

"We need to check bookings on the Cay."

Edward closed his diary and nodded. "Of course." Lucas thought he looked a little disappointed and wished he had worded it another way.

"Then you can add us to your diary," Dylan added. "Soon though, so Tasha can fly."

Edward nodded in enthusiasm.

"I have another toast," Lucas said. He looked directly at Dylan as he spoke. "This will mean very little to you all, but here's to Alfie and Peter."

Everyone dutifully copied the toast and Lucas and Dylan both sat down. Dylan curled a hand around his and squeezed tight. "Alfie and Peter," he repeated.

"I wonder what happened to Alfie."

"We'll find out in the new year."

When dinner was finished, they all repeated what had happened with last night's dishes. Each person, apart from Tasha, who was told to sit and enjoy what was left of the turkey, took plates and bowls to the kitchen, and as a group they cleared away under Adam's direction. Lucas strolled back into the dining room and took the chair next to Tasha.

"Think you'll be here next year? You and Liam and the little one?"

She tilted her head. "You sound sad, big brother. You worried you're going to miss out?"

Despite his objection to the Lamberts' kids, this was different. This was his little niece or nephew—blood. "Big time. I'd like to be a hands-on uncle..." He stopped talking. He'd made his life here and he was happy.

"Doesn't mean you can't spoil your niece or nephew

by internet. And think, he or she will be the only one in their class who gets to spend Christmas in the sun at Sapphire Cay."

"True. I'll make it to you for when the baby arrives." His reassurance was soft and she gripped his hand with tears in her eyes.

"I am so pleased you said that," she whispered back.

Lucas laughed. "I may faint though."

"I knew I could count on you doing that."

They hugged and Lucas was overwhelmed with emotion. Sadness, happiness, excitement, nerves, but the best of them all: love.

"Want to go outside for fireworks?"

JAMIE WAS IN CHARGE OF FIREWORKS, CITING HIS experience with ordnance and engineering. Lucas wasn't convinced that Jamie should be allowed near the damn things given the former Marine was entirely too comfortable setting off whole sequences of them. Admittedly, the gold and red against the ebony night was spectacular, but Lucas decided to keep his distance and had set up a nice safe area with Dylan up against the bar by the pool. Mutt sat next to them. They'd been worried that Mutt would be scared, but the dog was as happy as Jamie with the noise and chaos, wanting belly rubs as gold and silver cascaded out of the sky.

Lucas recalled something he'd meant to say. "Jamie

said he'd speak to his mom and dad about Alfie and Peter."

"Is that what you were chatting about earlier? You both looked serious."

"That and the fact he wanted to do the fireworks. I said he was only allowed to set off one at a time, and he said *he* was the ordnance expert and that *he* would be deciding what went off when. I just said I'd hide somewhere safe until I got the all clear." He chuckled as he explained.

Dylan smiled and stared up at the display. "He's good." He winced as two huge bangs were followed by a crash and fizzle of purple sparks high above them. "Maybe he can work with Edward on weddings."

"Chaotic weddings, maybe."

"That rules out one of Edward's, then."

They spent a long time kissing and talking weddings as best they could over the noise of the fireworks. Their wedding had been set for the first week of March when May fourth was shown to be too busy, and they had no say in anything except the vows. Apparently, Edward was looking after it all. Liam pulled a seat over next to them, and Tasha curled up on the soft seat and closed her eyes.

"Is Tasha okay?" Lucas asked Liam.

"Tired, but she didn't want to miss the fireworks, and yes I know she's asleep, but like she said, it's the thought that counts."

Next to join them from the beach were Edward, Scott, and Adam, who ranged out with the rest of them.

Finally, a grinning Jamie collapsed onto the sand.

"That was such a rush," he exclaimed, then spluttered when Mutt jumped on him. The two of them scrabbled in the sand and had everyone laughing.

The moment was a perfect mix of friends and fun.

---

LUCAS STOOD ON THE PIER. IT WAS THE MORNING AFTER Christmas Day and he wanted nothing more than to still be curled up in bed with Dylan.

Scott lifted the last of Edward's bags onto the *Liberty*. "How much do you actually carry around with you?" Scott griped as Edward climbed aboard and settled himself on the seat.

"I make up for Jamie," he said with a grin. True to Edward's assessment, Jamie sprinted down the beach and leaped onto the wooden jetty. More carefully, he made his way onto the *Liberty* and stowed his one flight bag in among Edward's Louis Vuitton cases.

"What you looking so prim about?" Jamie asked. He kissed Edward firmly on the lips, then shoved his lover to one side to get more seat space. Lucas observed how Edward pasted a fake annoyed expression on his face before grinning behind Jamie's back.

"Wondering how my big tough Marine is always late for everything," Edward teased.

"I was saying goodbye to Adam," Jamie defended.

Edward pressed a finger to Jamie's mouth. "I can see the cranberry sauce stains on your lips from here."

Jamie waggled his eyebrows. "Turkey sandwich."

Lucas chuckled. "For breakfast?" he asked.

Jamie patted his stomach. "Breakfast of champions."

Scott started the engine and fiddled with levers before wiping his hands on his worn jeans. "We ready to go?"

Lucas waved the three men away. Scott would be back later and Edward would be here for the Croft wedding. Jamie though, Lucas may well not see him for a couple of months.

Dylan came up behind him and held him close from behind.

"Were the turkey sandwiches good?" Lucas asked idly as the *Liberty* disappeared from view.

"How the hell did you know that?" Dylan defended.

Lucas turned in his hold and kissed his fiancé. "I know everything."

A loud woof gave them some advance notice of Mutt barreling into them, an event which concluded with Lucas in the shallows and Dylan lying on top of him. They grinned at each other while Mutt jumped on shells in the water then darted back when a wave smacked his nose.

"Ready to go back in?" Dylan asked as he stood. He held out a hand to Lucas who used the help to stand. He was soaked to the skin, but it didn't matter as he pulled Dylan in for a close hug.

Nothing else mattered except for Dylan being right here in his arms and the rest of his family being safe and well.

Mutt barked, then shook his fur until every molecule of sandy sea water was off of him and on Lucas and Dylan. Seemingly satisfied his job was done, he trotted back to the house and flopped down on the wide porch. Liam and Tasha were sitting there in the shade and Liam attached Mutt's long lead.

Dylan held out his hand, which Lucas took. "I'll get started on his run tomorrow. I promise."

"Meanwhile," Lucas sniffed the air. "I smell of dog. You smell of dog. We should go to the waterfall and wash off."

"We do have a shower, you know," Dylan smirked.

Lucas deliberately stated what he wanted. "You. Me. Naked. Waterfall. Shack. Now."

Dylan inhaled the early morning air and stretched his free hand above his head. Then the two of them fell in step toward their place.

*Alfie and Peter's place.*

Read the next book in Sapphire Cay - Capture the Sun

Capture the Sun (Sapphire Cay 5)

**The past has a powerful hold on Mitch, but meeting Isaac makes him desperate for a future filled with love.**

Isaac is desperate to break into the world of fashion design and be seen as something more than just an airhead model with no imagination. Set to debut his new collection, he has the models, the clothes. All he needs is a location, and he turns to an industry trouble-shooter for help.

Mitch's latest client needs an exotic location for a model shoot, and he happens to know someone with the very thing—Sapphire Cay. What starts as just another job turns out to be more exhilarating than winning any multi-million-dollar contract, particularly when he connects with Isaac again, who is far from the airhead model he presented as. As the fashion shoot gets underway, Mitch has to contend with complicated feelings for his old flame, Dylan, and the growing love he has for Isaac.

## Boyfriends For Hire

1. <u>Darcy</u>
2. <u>Kaden</u>
3. Gideon
4. Jared
5. Felix
6. Caleb

## Standalone Christmas

- <u>The Road to Frosty Hollow</u>

## Also from RJ & Meredith

### Standalone Christmas

- <u>The Road to Frosty Hollow</u>

### Free Reads

- Stronger Together

## Meet RJ Scott

RJ discovered romance in books at a very young age and realized that if there wasn't romance on the page, she could create it in her head. With over one hundred and fifty books published, she is a full time author of gay romance.

She lives and works out of her home in the beautiful English countryside, spends her spare time reading, watching films, and enjoying time with her family.

The last time she had a week's break from writing she didn't like it one little bit and has yet to meet a box of chocolates she couldn't defeat.

www.rjscott.co.uk | rj@rjscott.co.uk

**NEWSLETTER - rjscott.co.uk/rjnews**

## Meet Meredith Russell

Meredith Russell lives in the heart of England. An avid fan of many story genres, she enjoys nothing less than a happy ending. She believes in heroes and romance and strives to reflect this in her writing. Sharing her imagination and passion for stories and characters is a dream Meredith is excited to turn into reality.

www.meredithrussell.co.uk
meredithrussell666@gmail.com

facebook.com/meredithrussellauthor
x.com/MeredithRAuthor
instagram.com/miss_meredith_r